The Cathedral Dimension

Joseph Pesavento

Copyright © 2024 by Joseph Pesavento

Cover Art copyright © 2024 by Zach McCain.

All rights reserved.

No part of this publication may be reproduced, distributed, or transmitted in any form or by any means, including photocopying, recording, or other electronic or mechanical methods, without the prior written permission of the publisher, except as permitted by U.S. copyright law. For permission requests, contact the author. The story, all names, characters, and incidents portrayed in this production are fictitious. No identification with actual persons (living or deceased), places, buildings, and products is intended or should be inferred.

eBook ISBN: 979-8-218-41221-0

Paperback ISBN: 979-8-218-41220-3

Cover Art by Zach McCain

Edited and formatted by 360 Editing (a division of Uncomfortably Dark Horror).

Editor: Candace Nola

Contents

Praise for The Cathedral Dimension	V
Trigger Warning	VI
Dedication	VII
Prologue	1
1. Chapter One	3
2. Chapter Two	8
3. Chapter Three	11
4. Chapter Four	16
5. Chapter Five	20
6. Chapter Six	23
7. Chapter Seven	29
8. Chapter Eight	34
9. Chapter Nine	42

10.	Chapter Ten	48
11.	Chapter Eleven	62
12.	Chapter Twelve	80
13.	Epilogue	93
Acknowledgements		95
About Joseph Pesavento		97

PRAISE FOR THE CATHEDRAL DIMENSION

"The Cathedral Dimension is a Clive Barker-esque tale of mortals tangled up in the affairs of otherworldly elder gods. The setting is crazy fun and unique, and we are given a slew of terrifying and original denizens. Another tight, brutal, and entertaining release for Pesavento." - Megan Stockton, author of BLUEJAY

TRIGGER WARNING

WARNING:
This book contains extreme violence, transphobia, and a combination of both. This story is **NOT** a personal reflection of the author's views in any regard. Discretion is advised.

DEDICATION

For Bell. Forever my favorite little monster.

Prologue

Fall showed its fierce, chilly air after the summer heat died down. The people in neighboring towns brought out their light jackets and prepped their yards for extensive gatherings of thousands of colorful leaves. With the rush of pumpkin picking, spooky decorations, and the scenic beauty of the slow death of trees, the highway flooded day in and day out with those wishing to admire the fall foliage away from the hectic and plain city.

An eyesore remained prominent among the trees, and everyone couldn't wait to remove it from their view. The constant complaints from several town meetings, counties burdened by the monstrous atrocity, until the decision became unanimous. The time for the amusement park to be demolished had come. The fence was erected, bulldozers arrived, but even that was not enough to stop the gathering of curious trespassers or the ever-growing homeless population finding shelter below the once beautiful rides they rode in their teenage years.

Palisades Playland stood a staple in the neighboring towns for a strong forty years. Generations grew up riding the many roller coasters, one of which held a world record for twenty-nine years and enjoying the vast arcades and family fun the entire park provided. Once a park everyone went to all summer long, bringing not only money to the surrounding towns, but plenty of jobs for the teens wishing to do anything else but mow lawns.

Seldom a decline of attendance, nor anyone killed by a faulty ride. The park didn't have any issues regarding maintenance or power outages. In fact, the park ranked as one of the best in the country, always on the top ten of the best amusement parks. Roller coaster junkies frequented the park, helping to expand the reach and hype for the park. Sadly, one day after a successful morning and steady attendance, the ground beneath the park shifted, and trembled, before suddenly swallowing game booths and damaging dozens of ride supports.

The people escaped unharmed, but the stability of the rides became compromised and made it impossible to remain operational. The doors closed and never reopened. Eleven years later, the city council finally announced that the park was to be torn down and set the demolition date.

Chapter One

Dylan and Clyde drove up to the entrance which was consumed by thick vines and weeds weaving through the bars and fences since closing halted regular maintenance. Their obscured vision still allowed remnants of what they remembered as kids.

"Do you remember the last time you rode any of these rides?" Dylan wiped his mouth after swallowing a gulp of his canned drink.

"Most likely twelve years old, four or five days before the ground swallowed it whole."

Dylan pulled around the gate, blocking the entrance. The fence wobbled more than he expected. The giant *NO TRESPASSING* sign stood with equal instability in his firm grip.

"I don't think cops have been here in a long time. Goddamn shame, this isn't going to be here next week."

Clyde walked closer. "That's why you want to go tomorrow night? To take one last spin?"

Dylan gripped Clyde's shoulders. "We owe it to our childhood to say goodbye. This place never let me down. Won't tomorrow night either."

"Are you sure? Between the ground, hobos, and animals, seems to me like more danger than fun."

"That's why you have me as your friend, Clyde. To be the one to remind you that you have balls. You always forget them."

Clyde glared at Dylan. "Yeah, I don't have balls. Right. So how do we sneak in and what time are we doing it?"

"Gonna have to be late so we can sneak in. Low profile. I'll come back later and find a weak spot in the fence. Don't need you making me nervous while I figure it out."

Clyde walked toward the car. He stopped, returning to Dylan. "What are you going to tell Leah?"

Dylan and Leah had been dating for the last two years of college. Since being home, they began growing estranged between work and their ambitious career goals. Leah buried herself in her master's degree courses and Dylan found steady work through people needing computer repair and IT work. He wanted a more ambitious approach, like streaming or investing in a PC building video channel, but his parents didn't share the enthusiasm he did, knowing computers came in handy with everyone and everywhere.

Leah developed a streak of cancelled dates or time to hang out. It often led to arguments and going days without talking on the phone and relying on texting at a convenient time. On top of that, Ariel, Leah's childhood friend who recently transitioned, always hung around.

She took every free minute away from Dylan to make sure Ariel adapted to her new life as a woman.

"She's not going to care if I go or not. Besides, she's going away with Ariel in a few days."

"That's my point. Didn't she tell you she wanted to spend the next few days with you before she leaves?"

Dylan didn't want to admit it, but he had familiarized himself with being alone. Growing estranged from Leah resembled being single again, spending more time with Clyde.

"I can put it off until she gets back."

"Dude, why don't you talk to her about it? Clear the air?"

Dylan walked along the fence, starting his search early for weak spots. "I'd rather not receive an answer I don't want."

"Stalling the inevitable isn't going to make either of you…"

Clyde stopped talking when a car approached in the distance. He didn't spot where it came from, but it drove quicker than either of them wanted.

"Dylan, car!"

Dylan rushed to the driver's side faster than Clyde. They got in and drove it through a wooded path, burying their visibility beneath the thick branches and vines.

A security patrol passed through within seconds of Dylan moving the car. Not very attentive, the security guard appeared lost or careless. They waited several seconds before looking out and exiting the car.

"Okay, I'll sneak back in tonight. Are you sure you're free tomorrow night?"

"I am, but you need to spend time with Leah. It's for the best."

Dylan pondered, gazing into Clyde's eyes. "How about a bit of a bonding exercise? I'll invite her to come along with us. She's been wanting to do something daring. Help alleviate some of that college stress."

Clyde didn't want Leah coming along. He didn't like awkward confrontations, and the idea of them fighting and him getting stuck in the middle of it made him anxious. He never brought spouses along when hanging out with friends, so he often felt like a third wheel.

"I don't want to be in the middle of your bickering. Why don't we come back after they leave?"

"Good point. I'll invite Ariel too."

Clyde rolled his eyes. "Not what I meant, but fine. I can entertain her while you two talk."

"Anything else, or can we go?"

Clyde's eyeline met something startling. He jumped. "Jesus!"

Dylan turned to a group of homeless people gathered behind the gate, staring at the two.

"Sorry to disturb you. We're leaving," Dylan said.

"Do you wish to enter the cathedral? The Messiah rests but awaits the worshippers' devotion. Witnesses to the long travel are crucial to a successful ceremony." The tallest, who seemed to be the leader, gripped the chain-link fence.

"You two are pure. Able and ready for the events of our god!"

"Yeah, okay, buddy." Clyde turned to Dylan. "Let's go. I don't need these crackheads touching us and getting something on us."

Dylan and Clyde got into the car, but the homeless group stared at them until they left. Neither of them spoke about it again, but it sat in the pits of their stomachs until the end of the night.

Chapter Two

Dylan knocked on Leah's door. She had a brief window in the afternoon where she would be home alone and not invaded by her nosier than usual parents, who had taken an interest in her master's and made sure Leah did everything to keep up with her grades. Pushy parents furthered Leah's stress.

Leah opened the door. "Hey. Been cramming all morning. Excuse the appearance." Stained sweatshirt and messy hair didn't distress Dylan. He understood she had a lot going on. He followed her to her room. Open textbooks and enough notecards to fill a backpack covered her bed. Dylan moved some to the side.

"Dylan, careful! I'm studying those!" Leah grabbed the messy pile Dylan moved and pulled them into a deck, putting them by her pillow.

"Sorry, sorry. So, do you have plans tomorrow?"

She expressed no acknowledgement of what he said.

"Earth to Leah…"

"Sorry. A lot to cover before my test next week. Haven't had a chance to relax."

Dylan reached over and leaned into Leah's face. "Can I have a moment of your time, please?"

"Only a second, and then I need to finish."

Dylan grew irritated. "Why did you invite me in if you're not going to engage in conversation?"

Leah put her books down, clearly showing irritation on her face. "What, Dylan?"

"Clyde and I are going into Palisades Playland tomorrow. One more time before demolition. I'd like for you and Ariel to join us."

"You want me to come and risk being arrested with you in an abandoned amusement park that is days away from being destroyed forever? This has to be one of the stupidest ideas you've ever had."

Dylan gripped her hands. "You haven't had a break in weeks. Come out one time with all of us. If you want to leave, I'm not going to stop you. But I think if you care about this relationship, you can give up one night and bring your friend with you."

Leah closed her books and piled her index cards. Dylan recognized the turning point in her mood.

"Okay, Dylan. I'll go out with you. I hope you understand what you're doing. If you think exploring condemned property is something I'm going to be thrilled about, you're wrong. So, I'll entertain you and Clyde for one night. Then you and I will have a long talk about the future."

Leah's passive aggressive tone angered Dylan. He didn't respond, but got up and left. A further argument would've ruined plans. He wanted to make this relationship work on top of keeping his plans with Clyde. Saying goodbye to a piece of their childhood had become a necessity, and he would do it at whatever cost.

Dylan dialed Clyde's number. "Hey, dude. Leah and Ariel are in. Don't think we're getting enthusiasm. I'm not going to let it spoil our fun, though."

"Works for me. How did the conversation go?"

"I don't think it's getting any better soon. Going to keep at it." Dylan didn't want to come off as pathetic on the phone. He dug deep for stoicism, something missing when talking to his estranged girlfriend.

Clyde paused. "Before we meet up with the girls, can we talk about…"

"Clyde, we can talk about it after the park. Right now, I have to mend my situation with Leah. Okay?"

"Fine…" Clyde hung up.

Too many conflicts between Dylan and his friends, so maybe his idea of fun wouldn't be as enjoyable as he thought.

Chapter Three

Bulldozers and demolition signs already decorated the inside of the park when Dylan arrived. He managed to find an easily accessible rear entrance due to some of the fencing falling apart. Though risky, it appeared easy for them to take separate cars in case they got chased away by security or something happened to one of their cars. The unstable ground made them a little more cautious, so they entered the same way but parked a distance apart to maintain their exit strategy.

Dylan was pleased to see he was able to park his car perfectly behind the aged fence. He exited his car to find Clyde nearby, waiting to enter. He was happy to see Clyde hid his car in the same manner.

"Hey, where are the girls?" Clyde asked.

"On their way. I gave them instructions on how to enter. My soon to be ex-girlfriend is good with directions. She'll be fine."

Clyde stared with curiosity. "Soon to be?"

"Never mind. Had to fight to make her show up. I hope Ariel is more open to exploring this place."

Clyde nodded. They stared at one another, trying to avoid talking about the situation Clyde wanted to handle. Dylan moved his attention to the bright headlights.

One flash and the lights turned off. Leah sped in and slammed on the brakes underneath a low-hanging branch. Ariel exited first.

"Well, nothing like a fresh dose of whiplash. Hey guys." Ariel peered at the car and back at the two gentlemen, gesturing that Leah drove like a psychopath. Dylan and Clyde smiled.

Leah exited the car without a word. She opened the back door and shuffled around. Ariel and Dylan exchanged a confused expression regarding Leah's stalling.

The car door closed. "Why is everyone staring at me?"

"We're not. Waiting for you to be ready."

Leah gave a fake smile. She adjusted the strap on her camera and checked the lens.

"Glad you brought your camera, babe."

"If I'm going to be out here all night, I might as well make the best of it and document some of our finds."

Dyland nodded and checked Clyde and Ariel's reactions. "Seems fine with me. You guys cool with it?"

"Yeah," Clyde and Ariel answered.

Leah walked ahead, getting to the back entrance sooner than the other three. "Do we have a plan or not?"

"We can figure it out once we…"

The same group of homeless people blocked their way of entering. The leader gripped the chain-link fence. Several of the other group members had tattered, blood-stained clothing and had a variety of markings, from fresh wounds to missing fingers. The thick coat of grime on their skin mixed with the deep red shade made a black slime drip from their attire. The sludge caked some of them more than others.

"Holy shit. It's the same people from yesterday," Clyde said. "Hey, do you guys all live here? We only want to come in and take some photos."

The leader smiled, revealing his yellow stained teeth and sores covering his lip like holiday decorations.

"You won't need your camera to witness the truth this evening. The ceremony will begin tonight. Some of us will be an eternal sacrifice and some of us will be granted access. I will give my life for the great Messiah."

Leah turned to Dylan with concern. "Dylan, I don't think we should be exploring around these crackheads. This isn't safe."

A woman, missing most of her hair and one eyebrow, slid her hand into the fence. Only two fingers remained on her right hand, and her thumb was severed above the fingernail.

"Not to worry, my sweet. No harm will come to you. We are all servants to the great consumer. He will decide who is worthy. My gut tells me that you are the one he chooses. Such beauty. Yes, he will make you the new queen!"

"These people are insane." Ariel couldn't stop staring, but she spoke softly.

"Please, we only want to explore. This place meant a lot to us as kids. We won't go near any of your camps or stuff. We want to wander the park, explore some of the old buildings. Maybe climb on some of the rides. Relive some of the excitement. Understand?"

The leader pointed at an opening in the fence twenty feet away from where they stood.

"Please, enter through that gap in the fence. We will guide you to safe passage. It is an honor for you all to be here on this special night."

The four friends didn't respond but walked to the fence, with Leah leading the way.

"Last chance to turn back, everyone. Something tells me this is going to be more trouble than it's worth." Leah met eyes with all of her friends, none of whom appeared eager to leave. She shrugged, walking to the opening.

The homeless group stood single file along the left side of the entrance. The friends walked in, greeted with horrific smiles and gesturing hands. They stood beneath the giant PALISADES PLAYLAND sign that had weathered down to a wooden frame and minimal paint that resembled more of a greyed white. The ticket booth roofing was caved in and shattered glass sprinkled around the doors. The turnstiles were rusted over, and some had been bent from the excessive vandalism. It amazed Dylan that someone took the effort to do such a pointless act. He and his friends had made it this far, and he was enthusiastic to revisit everything he once enjoyed with his parents.

"Please, don't hesitate to find us if you need to cleanse your soul before the great one begins his ritual. Access is limited, so be sure to avoid any impure behavior."

Leah put her hand up to silence the missing finger lady. "Okay, what is this you're rambling about? Access to what?"

"The cathedral, of course, my dear. We are only here for a short amount of time. The cathedral, in the void beyond this world, is opening its doors to grant those who are worthy an entrance for everlasting fulfillment!"

She raised her arms in the air, showing all the friends how mangled her body had become.

"So, through here? That's it?" Clyde asked.

The homeless group nodded in unison.

The friends moved forward, not saying another word.

"Good luck, young friends! May the entrance be open to you all!"

Dylan waved with a smile, walking forward with his friends.

"What a fucking nutjob group," Leah said. "So, where are we going?"

Clyde shrugged. "That's the fun of it. We had nothing planned."

Leah's eyes rolled as she walked deeper into the park. None of them seemed scared by what the homeless group said, but tension resonated within the friends' presence.

CHAPTER FOUR

A strong silence among the group held prominent for the first ten minutes of wandering the overgrown grounds. Weeds towered through the concrete up to their knees. Most of the paint on the rides had worn down to a dull version of once vibrant colors. The tallest in the park, *Death's Infinity*, leaned and creaked dangerously toward the ground. Reports from the local news stated this would be the first ride to go once the demolition started. The ride falling on its own was a constant risk for the local fast-food restaurant that got the view of the giant ride right from the front entrance. The danger of debris breaking through the main window always concerned the townspeople.

The group of friends walked under the drooping steel monster, seemingly ready to collapse. Leah snapped photos before passing by the lowest hanging portion of the ride.

"So, Ariel, did you ever come here as a kid?" Clyde asked.

"A few times. Before I transitioned, of course."

Ariel was a different person before transitioning. Like a new student in school, always a quiet individual who seldom brought attention; it became obvious absence in abundant portions from school. Rumors stirred within the gossip filled halls. One or two people kept in touch, but only whispers were shared until word broke. The irony of a once timid kid not getting interaction with fellow peers, now the talk of the town because of a new identity. The sole transgender kid in the county now made you the most popular conversation among parents and children alike. Ariel, reborn into the new person she buried within herself, now free to the world. Though still young enough to be vulnerable, it didn't counter her confidence being her truest. Leah, someone who stood up for people, welcomed Ariel and they remained inseparable.

"Right," Clyde said. "Did you always want to be a girl?"

Ariel stopped, looking at Clyde.

"Want to be? No, it's who I've always been. I finally allowed myself to embrace it."

Because Ariel often faced bullying, Leah remained defensive of her, snapping at people for asking Ariel simple questions, despite being okay with answering for the sake of education. Dylan nudged Clyde, urging him to stop the current topic of conversation.

"I'm not trying to be rude at all, Ariel. I hope it's not coming off that way."

"I understand. I appreciate you considering my feelings with the topic. A lot of cis men don't consider how it may come off."

Clyde tilted his head. He appeared puzzled by the "cis" term.

"Guys!"

The congregation of squatters returned within the path. Now in the dozens. They surrounded Dylan and his friends.

"Dylan, fucking say something. I'm really not comfortable with them being so close to us! Go!"

Dylan stepped forward with Clyde shortly behind.

A shorter man, with a stump at the elbow and gashes in his neck, walked toward them.

"It has been a long time since we've had visitors outside of the vagabonds before you. What brings you to our holy land, travelers? Do you wish to be among the saved?"

Dylan stood before the man, who smelt worse than anticipated. His blackened teeth and breath revolted Dylan. He covered his nose; the man was practically intolerable to stand near. He could tell the man saw his disgust.

"Hello, I'm Dylan and these are my friends. We grew up coming to this place. Well, until it closed, obviously. Earthquake and all that."

"Oh, my sweet boy, no earthquake disrupted this holy land. The awakening, the great abysmal eyes opened and witnessed the light. Lost in the darkness, trapped beneath for all those long years. It has taken decades to find its following and belief in going back, and on this night it will return to the world it came from. It will be returning to the cathedral."

The others whispered and murmured as the mangled man spoke. They all gazed at Dylan, however.

"You're the second person to mention a cathedral. What is that? Like a church? A church on this property?"

The stumped arm touched Dylan's shoulder as the other arm gripped Dylan's opposite shoulder, releasing a foulness from his underarm. Dylan couldn't escape the disgusting aroma.

"This land, the entire plot that the people of this world blocked off, belongs to the being below. He will show us salvation and he will bring us along as we have devoted ourselves to him. You and your friends are the final pieces. You will unlock it. You will be the key to the grand doors. Now go, do as you wish to enjoy on this mortal land. Tonight, will be the final. The last for our time among mankind."

The filthy hand guided down Dylan's cheek and the man returned to the single file line his group formed. A pathway formed for the friends. The mangled and sickly people retreated to the depths of the park after the four walked ahead, still lost in the words spoken to them.

Chapter Five

Several rows of carnival games remained intact. Most of the prizes still hanging had either molded over from the weather or in ragged tatters of fuzzy fabric and dirty cotton stuffing. The center of the games, the one with the stacked bottles meant to be knocked down with a baseball, displayed heavy graffiti and showed evidence of various forms of aggressive battering. In the center, in bold red spray paint, read HE WILL FEED ON THESE GROUNDS. Beneath in black read AND RETURN TO THE CATHEDRAL, finished the bizarre mantra the friends recognized from the current inhabitants of the park all night.

"Ariel, can you help me reach this giant bear?" Leah asked.

"Sure." Ariel interlocked her fingers, taking a step toward her devoted friend.

Dylan walked ahead, keeping an eye on them. Clyde walked beside him, scanning the deteriorating games and surveying the distance for more disturbed inhabitants. Clyde's hand slid down Dylan's back.

"What are you doing?"

Clyde's hand retreated. "They aren't looking. It's okay."

"Clyde, I don't want to do this now. We can talk about it later."

"Can't we talk about what happened? I need some clarity on what it means and what you want."

Dylan stopped Clyde, facing the girls to make sure they don't become suspicious.

"Clyde, we have enough on our plate right now between Leah on the verge of leaving me and homeless people killing us before the night ends. Can we please hold off on discussing things? I promise you tomorrow we will talk about everything. Can we do that?"

Dylan could tell Clyde was leaning toward tears before nodding and walking ahead. He resented withholding the closure Clyde wanted given what happened between them several nights ago, while the drinking escalated further than both anticipated. Still, Dylan wanted to keep his mind focused on giving his best to Leah, despite the situation not showing promise in his favor at the moment.

A loud crash echoed as Leah fell to the concrete and the structure supporting the carnival game gave out to the years of rust. The folding metal rang into the air for what sounded like hours.

Ariel pulled Leah to her feet. They burst into hysterical laughter while Leah dusted herself off.

"Leah! Are you okay?" Dylan grabbed her around the waist. Leah resisted Dylan's physical contact.

"Yeah, I'm fine." She walked ahead of Ariel. "I think we should split up into twos. Cover more ground that way."

Dylan, planning on trying to use this evening to bond with Leah and Ariel, saw that it had backfired for him. Her lack of eye contact while speaking gave him the indication that she was trying to sabotage his efforts to improve their situation.

"I agree. Girls and boys' groups!" Ariel gripped Leah's arm.

"You're serious? You want to go out on your own with a bunch of creepy dudes hiding in the darkness?" Clyde got in front of Dylan, questioning Leah's capabilities.

"Gee, I suppose big strong boys would be a better fit for wee little girls like us." Leah pulled out a taser, clicking it on, startling Clyde with the loud hum. "I think we will be fine with twenty thousand volts. I also gave Ariel bear mace. We're set. "

"Leah, I wanted this night to be for all of us, not a game of hide and seek. Why don't we all stay together?" Dylan extended his hand.

Leah pushed past Clyde and Dylan, guiding Ariel with her. She ignored his question.

"Leah!"

"Dylan, you're a big boy. You and your boyfriend can survive for at least an hour without me protecting you. Here." Leah tossed him a walking talkie. "Scream if you need me to save you."

Leah and Ariel vanished into the darkness. Dylan and Clyde made eye contact, and Dylan broke it by walking ahead. Dylan followed behind. They pondered on where to go next.

Chapter Six

Dylan and Clyde decided to walk the wooden bridge path toward some of the smaller rides. Despite most of the bigger rides having a better aesthetic, these provided plenty more to explore; rides they could climb without having to risk their lives. Some of the smaller entrances meant for employees and maintenance weathered to the point of serving no purpose or could be easily pushed in without much effort. Despite being vacant for over ten years, much more decay seemed evident, which confused them both.

"Weird that some of these rides look like they've been here for fifty years rather than eleven. Did you notice that?" Dylan asked.

Clyde pushed on a wall, toppling over as it fell to the ground. Some squatters ran out from behind, rushing into the darkness.

"Tonight is the night!"

"Fucking creeps scared the shit out of me." Clyde pushed on the collapsed wall with his shoe. "Yes, that's odd. Like aging here in the park sped up somehow."

Dylan climbed out and gazed down the row into the blackness. It was quieter than expected, given the hundreds of people that took refuge in the park every night. A familiar ride, *Endless Cavern*, reared its decrepit aged doorway just ahead of them. A ride, designed like a cavern exploration journey, populated with monsters hiding in the rocks. It was one of the more popular attractions of Palisades Playland. The scare factor worked into the more stylized rides kept attendees coming back for more.

"Hey, Clyde, do you remember Endless Cavern?" Dylan pointed at the entrance.

Clyde walked past Dylan. "Of course! My favorite one! I'd go on this ride three to four times a day!"

Clyde stopped just before entering. He admired the hard hat light overhead that gave some visibility to the macabre entrance. A bulb, long burnt out and far from recovering, he stared up at the wiring protruding from the fixture that his childhood self remembered like he was still attending.

"It's much creepier without the overhead light, don't you think?"

"We'll be fine. Those creepy people aren't dangerous. They're just trying to find food and shelter. I think Leah is more paranoid than anything." Dylan clicked his flashlight on to admire the wiring and fill the absence the hard hat decor once lit.

Clyde stepped into the empty cavern attraction first. "Women. They are always more paranoid."

After several steps, Clyde slipped, gripping the wall before tumbling down to the ground. A pool of blood soaked the floor, drenching his clothing. He tried to stand, but struggled from a lack of grip.

"Dude, help me!" Clyde extended his hand, waving it in a panic. Dylan reached out, pulling Clyde to his feet. He backed away once the dripping red covering Clyde's entire torso and halfway down his jeans touched his own skin.

"Damn, did you hurt yourself?" Dylan checked Clyde's body. He didn't have any wounds.

Clyde's face went pale. It was the most scared Dylan had ever seen him.

"This isn't my blood."

Clyde pointed toward the cavern entrance. Dylan followed the almost black fluid, drenching the floor until visibility evaded the end of the pool; the darkness took over the deeper depths.

"Happen to catch anyone else inside? Or an animal?"

Dylan clicked on his flashlight. The thick pool of blood went deep into the attraction entrance, further than visible, without walking toward the mess.

"No, but it's fresh. Whatever happened, just happened. Maybe we should find the ladies and leave."

A loud snap echoed out of the cavern, startling them both. They stared into the blackness.

A man dressed in baggy clothing stood just far enough from the corner to reveal himself. His smile was unsettling to Dylan. Clyde's face showed equal dread.

"Hey."

"Um... hello." Dylan stepped back, getting closer to Clyde.

"How are you?" The man's question seemed emotionless. It was as if the man was a prerecorded message.

"Hey, um, are you okay? This blood on the ground... Looks like it just happened."

A long pause followed before the stranger responded. He wiped his nose, pulling a string of mucus from his moist nostril. It dangled down to his lip before his tongue crept out to suck it down, hack, and spit into the red pool.

"We all lose blood in this place. Hard to keep track of who it belongs to."

Dylan thought something was peculiar about this individual aside from the rest of the bizarre behavior going on with the park's inhabitants. This man was being more suspicious than the others. The need to hide in the darkness without moving was unsettling. The hairs on the back of Dylan's neck stood up.

"Who are you? Why are you hiding?" Clyde asked as he crept inside.

Dylan grabbed his arm. He shook his head at Clyde.

The man's hand lunged forward, slapping against the wall he hid behind. He dragged what few fingers remained against the wall. A mixture of what appeared to be blood and grime smudged the wall as the hand slid down and fell back to his side.

"This here is my home. I ain't leaving my home for no one. Not s'pose to."

"What do you mean, you're not supposed to?" Dylan asked.

The man hugged the wall. Clyde stepped back as the man's glare pierced through them both.

"This here is where I live. This cave. Ain't leaving for nothing."

Dylan tapped Clyde. "Let's leave. This guy is giving me the creeps."

Clyde nodded. "Right."

"Sir, you have a great night and enjoy your home." Dylan waved and turned to walk away.

"Wait!" the man yelled.

Clyde and Dylan turned to see a dark green appendage reaching out for them. It extended back to the man, who had stepped forward into the brightness enough for them to witness the green extension coming from the man's torn open forearm. The teeth, now appearing abnormal once Dylan took the time to pay attention to them as he smiled, were fine and razor like.

"Lied to you. Think he can answer for the blood."

The green appendage retracted and grabbed something from the other side of the wall. A loud splash hit the ground in front of the two, dowsing their jeans in a dark crimson. A mass of shredded skin and clothing, like deer roadkill, was sprawled out in front of them. The face was caved in and mangled, unrecognizable. The throat protruded through torn open neck and the torso resembled a cherry dessert turned inside out. The clothing interwove between the various gashes around the body.

Clyde bent over, dry heaving, while Dylan stepped back from the lasagna-like man.

"Clyde, let's go!" Dylan pulled at him while running away. He only glanced back to ensure his friend was behind him. After getting a few yards away, they saw the man emerge from the darkness of the ride, the green appendage waving as he smiled.

Dylan couldn't tell if the man was more human or creature, but he refused to wait around to find out.

They ran, not entirely sure which direction they were headed. The darkness heightened their fear, but the mutated man lingered on in their heads.

Chapter Seven

After a few minutes of running, Dylan and Clyde slowed down and caught their breath. The view in front of them was the decaying carousel with several horse heads removed and several more knocked over altogether. The back of the ride was black, not giving any view of what may lurk in the depths. Dylan tried to find anyone nearby; not wanting to have any more surprises coming their way. Clyde struggled for air more than Dylan did.

"What… What the fuck was that?" Clyde asked.

Dylan had no idea. He didn't have an answer that would suffice, anyway. For a moment, Dylan pondered the thought of falling at some point during the night and the horrors inhabited his thoughts as part of the trauma from a head injury. Gallons of blood flooding the entrance of a ride guarded by a man with an arm or appendage stretching more than ten feet? Didn't seem like something that could break into his reality.

"I'm just as confused as you are." The night seemed to swallow them further. The stars appeared dimmer than when first entering the park.

"What do we do now?" Clyde asked.

Dylan pulled the walkie talkie from his pocket. After the attitude and vibe Leah gave, he didn't think reaching out was a great idea. After all, he believed as if he needed her more than she needed him. The change in behavior toward their relationship weighed on him, and he wanted to enjoy the night exploring a soon to be memory of his childhood.

"I'll check on the ladies." Dylan clicked the radio on. "Not sure if their night is as weird as ours. But I need to encourage them to leave."

"Dylan…" Clyde crossed his arms.

"Yeah?" Dylan asked, still staring at the walkie talkie, replaying the thoughts of Leah letting the relationship fail.

"Leah isn't the right person for you." He placed his hand on the walkie. "Not by a long shot."

"Clyde, we don't need to do this right now. Please." Dylan hesitated to call her. He didn't have much confidence left in making it work since Leah put in almost no effort as of late.

Clyde grew impatient toward the hesitation to call. "Can you bring yourself to do it? I've convinced you too."

"Enough. Just fucking stop already." He switched channels, remembering which channel Leah asked him to use.

"Leah, where are you ladies?"

No answer.

"Leah. Where are you two?"

The walkie's static was the only sound echoing in Dylan's ears. It rang, over and over again, and he swore a presence surrounded him. Growing bigger and overwhelming him.

"BOO!"

Dylan jumped, turning around to find Ariel smiling behind her poorly applied makeup. She was still learning the proper technique, as make-up was new to her.

"Jesus fucking Christ, Ariel!" Dylan bent over, breathing in deeply.

Leah turned the corner, looking behind her while approaching Dylan and Clyde.

"Damn, I got you good," Ariel gloated while giving Leah a high five. "Boys are always so scared."

Leah nodded.

Clyde scoffed. "Easy scare. You're still a noob at it."

Leah sorted through her bag. "You chumps catch anything good? These people are quite the graffiti artists."

Clyde and Dylan exchanged a glance, debating if they should share the experience with the deformed man and his bizarre appendage. Leah and Ariel wouldn't believe them, anyway.

"Just a lot of weirdo homeless people," Clyde said.

Clyde's comment caught Dylan off guard. He was ready to pack it in after their experience. He was trying not to make it obvious to everyone how shaken up he was, but his gut was telling him to take everyone to their cars and call it a night.

"What made them weird?" Leah asked.

Clyde shrugged. "Quite filthy and asking us a bunch of weird questions."

"What makes them filthy? It's not their fault they can't have access to proper hygiene."

Ariel chimed in. "Clyde, you should educate yourself on people who don't have your white privilege. Not everyone acquires what they want whenever they want it."

Clyde and Dylan hesitated, sensing the tension growing, but didn't speak up. Clyde's demeanor often bested Dylans when it came to speaking up and out. He didn't want to cross a line by ruining the night or insulting one of the girls.

"First of all, you're white, too, and I think just about every person in this park we've encountered has been white. Not sure why that's important, anyway."

"But not all white males. Myself and a few women we encountered don't have what you can gain with ease."

Clyde's eyes narrowed. "But you transitioned. You chose to have less accessibility. Your words, not mine. No need to act high and mighty because you want to be a girl."

Ariel's jaw dropped. Leah stepped in Clyde's face, punching him hard just below the collarbone.

"Fucking apologize, you dickhead. Don't you ever misgender her in front of me again."

Clyde rubbed at his soreness. "Fuck you, you didn't need to hit me."

Ariel turned to walk away. "This is what I have to deal with every day of my life. Typical that you wouldn't understand."

Leah could tell the sniffling would lead to sobbing within the next few minutes. She followed, but stopped briefly to address her boyfriend and the friend she regretted joining tonight.

"Leah, I'm sorry. Clyde didn't mean it. Can we just head back—"

"Nice, Dylan. Way to have a friend like that getting in the way of tonight. That's not something I can look past. Take a walk and call me when you got your priorities in line."

Leah shot a look at Clyde. "I'm getting an apology out of you by the time the sun comes up. For your sake."

She walked off, leaving Clyde and Dylan in the darkness.

A loud eruption of laughter echoed after Leah vanished. Dylan turned to a homeless man, missing both legs, sitting at the foot of the carousel. He propped himself upright with his frail arms riddled with deep scars.

"Ah ha ha! Better straighten up, boy! She is the one to lead us back! If you want to be king, you gotta make that shit right!"

Dylan waved Clyde over, walking away from the laughing man. They couldn't escape the laugh even after he fell deeper in the darkness. They kept going, but the sound followed for a little while.

Chapter Eight

Clyde's comment caught Dylan off guard. He didn't expect something so transphobic out of his friend. A first time Clyde ever mentioning an issue with someone who transitioned. Clyde loved to call people out for rude behavior or talking shit, but this was beyond Dylan's comprehension of cruelty.

The two walked further into the darkness in silence. Clyde was looking down at the ground while he walked. Dylan searched around for anything else unusual, but nothing besides the occasional vagabond smiling and to reveal stained teeth on the verge of falling out.

"So, you definitely went too far before with Ariel. That shit doesn't fly well, Clyde."

Clyde scoffed. "That's Leah talking. Not you."

Dylan stopped in front of his agitated friend, putting a hand up to stop Clyde from walking further.

"I'm serious. That was a dick head move."

Clyde waved Dylan away. "She'll forget it. It's not like it's a real thing for her. She lacked prejudice in her life until she transitioned. I'm tired of pretending she had some difficult life because one day she decided she was different. I, on the other hand, have struggled, and I'm not going to pretend it's less important because I'm not trans myself."

Dylan didn't have any other words at the moment. He thought about Ariel prior to the transition. Often quiet, a person who seldom spoke in school, an individual you probably couldn't recognize if you bumped into them on the weekend at the mall or somewhere else you've been a thousand times. She may have struggled prior to becoming Ariel, but otherwise, all signs pointed to someone who would simply disappear into the wave of normality.

"Like we call her Ariel, but do you remember her name before that? I'm only calling her Ariel because I can't recall her previous name."

"Dude, you need to stop. I wanted to fucking leave and now we're wandering for some strange reason. We need to find them and apologize to them both."

Clyde gripped Dylan. "No, you need to face the elephant in the room and address what I've been trying to for days now. We need to talk about what we did."

"Clyde…" Dylan pointed behind his friend. Standing over six feet was a mangled man, still able to work up a smile that Dylan didn't quite understand. The flesh of his cheek was shredded, displaying his gums and teeth. A gash spread from the base of his ear down to the top of his exposed biceps. His torn shirt drooped down to his waist. He waved, displaying a hand sparse of fingers.

"Evening, my fair gents. Name's Norman. How you doing tonight?"

Dylan eyed the tattered nature of this man, pondering how he was able to stand with such dismay about his build. The more he examined the wounded man, the more life-threatening injuries appeared.

The man spat a red wad from his mouth. "You both part of the ceremony?"

"What is that? Why does everyone in here keep referring to a ceremony or ritual? What the fuck is going on?" Clyde's aggravation startled Dylan. A breaking point was imminent.

He raised his arms. More scars were apparent in the dim light. "The servers guide us back to their world! You will be part of the opening as we all part with life on Earth! They asked us to set the stage for worthy travelers, and here you are! You two and the ladies going about the Ferris wheel a few hundred yards that way."

The man pointed with his severed index at the crumbling Ferris wheel. Three of the higher carts had fallen to the ground and stood in the sky like a broken wheel. It still maintained colorful vibrance throughout the standing carts.

"Who are the makers?" Dylan asked.

He walked toward the two, revealing the only two teeth in his mouth. "You met one in the cavern, but he was a hybrid. His devotion let him cross over. Survived it at least. There's more of them out there. The makers are among us. In the walls, in the ground." He leaned into earshot of Dylan. "Hell, the Messiah caused the damn park to collapse. It was he who found this world and has been trying to return ever since. He ain't letting anyone out tonight if these fine creatures can leave and be on our way home."

"The Messiah?" Clyde and Dylan said in unison.

"Only he can open the cathedral doors. The one in charge. Big motherfucker too. He needs enough blood to keep himself full for the travel. Any minute now, he's going to make another person worthy of entering his domain."

He pointed to the sky. Dylan and Clyde waited for something to happen. The air grew quiet, as if on queue. That overwhelming stress hit Dylan again. Like darkness lurked around them, making the night impossible to escape. It wasn't long before a distant sound echoed in the air. A bear or a coyote. He couldn't quite make it out.

Then it appeared.

A similar appendage, which now resembled more of an arm, grew into the night sky like something stretching after a long rest.

The roar came again, but mightier than before. Not a bear, nor a coyote. A colossal being that Dylan had never experienced before.

Something not from this world; not an animal at all.

The appendage swung down like a scorpion's stinger, piercing the mangled man through his gut. Warm red sprayed across Dylan's shirt and Clyde's neck. Clyde immediately started to gag while shouting at the same time.

"Ahh, it is my time! I'll see you at the altar!"

Blood flowed from the man's lips as he went airborne, returning to the source of the appendage's location. He was pulled out of sight, and the silence took over once more.

The roar returned.

Mightier than before. A creature of massive size. A beast more powerful than anything this planet could offer.

"Clyde, we need to take the girls out of here. Right now."

Dylan couldn't shake the impending doom that was lingering all around him. Something unnerving about this threatening presence. A growing sense of danger overshadowed the darkness of night, and it grew stronger every second they stayed in the park.

"So, we're bailing?" Clyde asked.

Dylan nodded at Clyde before rushing toward the gate they came in from. Clyde matched his pace quickly.

Dylan pulled out the walkie, clicking it on. "Leah, it's time to leave! Stuff is getting weird out here. Meet us at the entrance!" The urgency burst from his lungs in between breaths.

No answer. *She has to be mad at us still. Leah was always one to ignore me when she was angry.*

"Leah? Ariel? Come in."

Nothing. Dylan grew angry, gripping the walkie, wanting to crush it with every bit of force. He was growing fearful, not sure if they were in danger or not.

"LEAH! Fucking answer me!"

Clyde pulled the walkie from Dylan's hand. "Let's get back to the car. Once we're closer, we can try again. We can look for her along the way."

"Fine."

Dylan and Clyde ran toward where they remembered walking in. The presence of the mangled attendees was absent. After thinking over how the one man was grabbed and pulled to his unknown demise, it seemed to be especially quiet around the once merry theme park.

Clyde made eye contact on and off throughout their quiet run. Dylan was growing further frustrated in the constant staring while running away from this dreadful night's events.

"Dude, why do you keep staring at me?"

"You've been avoiding the answer to that question all night."

Dylan ran faster, ignoring the now grinning Clyde staring at him more. He kept thinking about the unworldly creatures that inhabited the cavern and the one that grabbed the mangled man in front of him. The gallons of unidentified blood still gave him chills. Something beyond his comprehension of reality was going on, and he had enough of it to want to dive into answers. He was ready to say goodbye to the park after what was going on.

Static erupted from the walkie, startling Dylan. He grabbed it out of Clyde's hand.

"Hey, Leah? You both okay?" Clyde asked.

Static responded with faint dialogue coming through.

"Leah? Hello, Leah."

"Dylan…over…end…not working…better…you…"

Dylan didn't need to figure out the rest of it to answer how she thought. The sinking in his chest confirmed he was ready to leave.

He grabbed the walkie from Clyde. "If that's your final thought, Leah, just leave it at that. You and Ariel can find your own way out of the park. Clyde and I are leaving! Goodnight."

The walkie clicked off and Dylan threw it as far as he could. It vanished into the blackness, and he wouldn't wait for it to explode on the ground or against a crumbling structure.

"Dylan, wait!"

"Fucking bitch! I make all this effort, invite her, and she can't be bothered. She should've just dumped me last night and you and I could've had a fun time by ourselves. Ariel probably doesn't like exploring like this!"

"Dylan…"

They approached the entrance of the park, unguarded like their grand arrival. The hole in the gate was not blocked by eager hosts. Dylan slipped right through, and Clyde followed right after.

He reached for his keys and Clyde gripped his wrist, trying to ease his nerves.

"Dude, just take a breath. She's not here at the moment."

Dylan paced in front of the car, taking in the events of the night. All the horrors that he endured were still insignificant to Leah's words. It crushed him, brought him down to a level he never thought Leah could bring him.

"I've done all I can, and it's still not enough. I can't bring myself to enjoy this. I can't pretend to be okay while she's ready to throw in the towel and not even confront me about it first! Fuck it all. I'm done caring."

He paced back and forth, then stopped abruptly. It came across his head. The thing he was avoiding.

"What is it?" Clyde asked.

"Hop in the back seat. Let's do it again. I need us again."

Chapter Nine

TWO WEEKS EARLIER

Clyde's parents had left for the weekend for much needed time alone. Clyde took the opportunity to let the house be swallowed by the mess of takeout, convenience store litter, and a pile of laundry that would grow until the very last minute. He had Dylan over for some weed in the basement. Dylan had purchased a case of beer to accompany the smoking venture they were sure to set sail on.

After some much-needed indulgence, the giggling had ensued. Clyde's high laugh, as Dylan called it, was squeakier than ever. It always got high pitched when the substances started going full swing.

"Dude, I thought you and your dad had sorted out that missing testicle problem. That voice needs some work."

Clyde coughed while inhaling another pass from the joint. "Fuck you, dude. I laugh like this when I'm high."

"Why is that?" Dylan asked.

"Because I don't smoke with no one else, idiot!" Clyde blew smoke in Dylan's face.

The two of them rarely enjoyed weed with one another. Dylan's mom hated the stench, and his dad was militant, no smoking of any kind. He never found out because he only did it at Clyde's. His parents hated it too, so he only did it when they were gone for more than two days. Clyde planned enough ahead to rid the aroma from the house. Plenty of time to blow fans and keep doors open. The perks of not having pets to run wild with doors left unattended.

"What else do you want to do tonight? There's a few good movies streaming that I want to check out."

"Ehh." Clyde coughed, not satisfied with that answer.

"Okay. Want to order in and blast some music?"

"Warmer, but not quite."

Dylan rolled his eyes. "So, what do you want to do?"

Clyde reached in, kissing Dylan on the lips. A second or two passed before Dylan broke the interaction.

"Whoa. Dude. What the fuck was that?"

Clyde slid a finger across his lips, wiping Dylan's excess saliva.

"Sorry. Wanted to try. Did you like it?"

Dylan and Clyde had been friends since middle school. Neither of them had ever discussed homosexuality other than the rampant insults they gave one another while gaming online. Dylan had never had any ambition to be with a guy before. He was fairly certain of his sexuality.

Once in a while, while indulging in porn, he pondered the craving of penis while watching his favorite stars devour it like it was a baked delectable. Besides that, his sexual desires were for Leah.

"I didn't realize you wanted me like that. It's cool and all, but I'm with Leah."

"Well, we've been friends for years. Any interest in just experimenting and seeing where it goes? I'm not going to tell anyone. I'm aware of the massacre that would lead to your social life in school."

"And with Leah…"

Clyde rolled his eyes. "Right."

"For the record, I'm just curious."

Clyde's eyes widened. He reached in, kissing Dylan intensely. Their lips locked, escalating the intertwining of their tongues. Clyde sat on Dylan's lap as their saliva danced between their mouths. Clyde grew erect, poking against Dylan's stomach. Dylan broke the kiss, taking in air and calming down from the heightened experience.

"Maybe we should dial it down a bit, Clyde."

Clyde shook his head. He was immersed in it and didn't want to halt the experience. He rubbed his hand over Dylan's groin. He wasn't as aroused, but Clyde kept going. He was ready to give it a shot, no matter how much he would have to beg.

Clyde's hand slid under Dylan's shorts, reaching in and taking in a handful of his flesh. Dylan let out a faint moan, already rising to meet his friend's touch with growing excitement as blood rushed to his throbbing dick.

It was less than a second after that Dylan's stiffness emerged from his shorts and into Clyde's mouth. His good friend had never revealed his sexual desires for guys, let alone his best friend, but Dylan had a rising suspicion that Clyde had done this before. His ability, motion, technique, and devotion were beyond what he had experienced before. Dylan's eyes rolled back as he let his friend pleasure him.

Time escaped the two of them. Clyde lived out his lingering fantasy as Dylan absorbed every drop of euphoria he was granted. Neither of them wanted to interrupt this.

Dylan's mind went elsewhere. Early hints of his disconnection from Leah, like less effort to have sex or hang out with him, made any sort of enjoyment between the two seem like work for her.

Clyde's talents far exceeded Leah's, but also exceeded her willingness to please. He didn't want to budge at all when it came to letting this new sensation go the distance.

Clyde's slurping of pre-cum and his own drool were drawing Dylan closer to his grand release. It grew. Every second he was inching toward a grand finish that had been absent for a long time.

Clyde took him all in, gliding down his throat. The lack of hesitation and resistance as the entire shaft slid deeper into his mouth sent waves of pleasure. Dylan's legs shook.

"Fuck, fuck!" Dylan held Clyde's head, filling his mouth with warm fluid. His eyes rolled back into his head, expressing a sexual satisfaction that he had only experienced one or two other times with such intensity.

He laid back, watching his friend ponder if the thick release in his mouth should be swallowed or spit.

Clyde swallowed it down, showing his bare tongue for approval.

"I thought it would be nastier. Not that bad."

Dylan slid his shorts up. "Where the hell did that come from?"

Clyde shrugged. "I guess I'm hornier when I'm a little buzzed. But I guess the secret is out now."

"I'll say." Dylan stood up.

"Wait, are you leaving?" Clyde asked.

"Is that a problem?" Dylan put his coat on.

Clyde stood, confusion all across his face.

"I'm sorry. Am I like a one-night stand to you? We're best friends. I reveal an extremely personal side of myself to you and you're just going to bounce?"

Dylan shook his head. "It's not that at all. My head is all over the place with the weed, the drinking. Leah…"

Clyde scoffed. "Of course."

"Look, I'm not going to say anything. I enjoyed it. I'm not really sure where I stand with this all. Just give me some time to think about it and we will figure it all out. Does that work for you?"

Clyde nodded. He faced away from Dylan. "Catch you later, I guess."

Dylan nodded. Without saying goodbye to his friend, he walked upstairs and left. Before entering the car, he checked his phone, showing a smiling Leah and himself on their first trip together.

Dylan texted her.

"You still awake?" he asked.

The three-dot icon appeared for several seconds. Then it vanished.

The moon icon appeared, indicating to Dylan that her notifications were silenced.

"Great." Dylan slid his phone in his pocket and started his car.

As he drove the short distance home, he thought about the dynamic between himself and Clyde and then himself and Leah. Would it be all that awful to devote himself to Clyde? Inseparable childhood friends, and often had more fun together than he and Leah ever did. It was his first sexual experience with a guy, and a good guy at that. He never really thought about sex with men outside of pornography, but he was pleased his experience was with someone he could trust entirely to keep it private if they didn't want to pursue a relationship and keep that part of themselves out of the public eye.

After all, some local people they grew up with didn't take kindly toward gay men.

Once inside, Dylan grabbed a snack and sat at his computer for a little while. After the buzz wore off, he lay in bed, thinking over the events of the night.

He couldn't recall who reigned in his mind. Clyde or Leah.

Either way, he had a lot of decisions to make going forward.

Chapter Ten

Dylan pushed Clyde against the passenger door while their tongues intertwined. They had momentarily forgot the terror and dove head first into something they'd avoided for too long. Clyde gripped Dylan's face and Dylan's explored his friend's body.

"So sorry. Sorry for putting this off," Dylan said. "God, your body feels good."

"Dylan, shut up."

Clyde reached for the door handle and opened the car. He climbed in and Dylan closed the door behind him before returning to Clyde's lips.

They were latched onto one another, incapable of letting go. Weeks of tension built up was quickly rising to the surface.

Everything felt normal once again. Despite the circumstances and the current relationship turmoil, everything felt right to them as they embraced the desires they could finally express in the privacy of their backseat.

Dylan slid his pants down, catching Clyde off guard. "Wait, what are you doing?"

"I need to feel your mouth again."

Dylan had his pants off by the time Clyde sat up. He was stroking, getting himself stiff for the task at hand. Clyde, still a bit flustered from the gore and human sacrifice of earlier, hesitated, given the circumstances.

Dylan had avoided the entire experience since it happened. He was often dismissive or distant from Clyde in hopes of keeping the awkward discussion minimal. He kept it from Leah. Unsure if her response would be to explode about the situation or worse, tell all his family and friends that Dylan was gay now. Not how Dylan had thought of himself, but he didn't let himself think it over, either. He buried the thoughts while trying to make it work with Leah.

Dylan stroked his stiff member, eyeing Clyde. "Well, isn't this what you wanted? I'm totally ready for it now."

"How on earth do you expect me to suck you right now after seeing all that blood with that mutated man, someone impaled right in front of us, and an ungodly sound come from somewhere in the park?"

Clyde did keep staring at Dylan's penis, enticing Dylan to keep stroking.

"I'm sure you'll love it once you start. Come on. You were just kissing me, anyway."

Clyde shook his head. "Pull your pants up."

"Dude, can you just…"

A blood-curdling scream echoed from within the park. Dylan and Clyde looked at each other for a moment.

"Leah!" Dylan pulled up his pants and hopped out of the car.

"What do we do?" Clyde asked. "We have no idea where that came from."

"We gotta find them either way. If I were to look, I'd guess Leah would be somewhere close to the middle."

"Let's go!"

Dyland and Clyde ran back inside. Several of the homeless that lingered around stood in single file with their select groups. They bowed at the two while they ran past.

"It has begun! The messiah wakes!" the group said in unison.

"Clyde, don't give them your attention. We find the ladies and bounce. Nothing else. Understood?"

"You don't have to tell me, dude. I'm fucking done with this place. Straight back to the cars at full fucking speed."

The population of deformed people was quickly escalating. They emerged from the shadows, gathering in small groups of four or five. They began to raise their left hands into the air.

"No matter what they do, just ignore them," Dylan said.

Dylan's mind was going at full speed, focused only on finding Leah. He recognized her scream, hearing it several times, either when a bug crawled past her feet or the select times that she'd agreed to a roller coaster. Dylan hoped she'd go to a central spot that would allow her to have a vantage point from all sides.

Then it occurred to Dylan.

"Dude, the opening in the ground! Where the sinkhole is? That's where she's going to be!"

"You think so? What makes you so sure?" Clyde asked.

"She'd want to understand why this place closed. I think it's the only real reason she came."

They raced toward the center of the park. The opening was located where the grand fountain stood. It was the highlight of the park and where people took the most pictures. It gave a scenic view of the taller rides and displayed the park's emblem embedded in the brick and concrete floor. A grand pair of cursive P's were on display for everyone entering the park. Most had to set their trip itinerary around the least amount of traffic so they could grab an iconic photo before leaving for the day.

Upon arrival, the cracked cement and fragmented brick were still visible before the opening. The hole was too deep for the bottom to be visible. The depth engulfed the opening in blackness. The night sky was but a fraction of darkness compared to the pit below.

"Jeez," Dylan said as he stopped before falling into the abyss. "That's fucking massive."

The absence of light made it harder to tell where the opening ended on the other side. It formed a trapezoid-like shape. Dylan found that unusual for something like an earthquake to make. Could it have been the integrity of the foundation being so strong that it didn't just open like a pit down to hell? It was unlikely, but Dylan didn't want the shape to distract him from what could very well be the entrance to the fiery depths.

"Leah! Ariel!" Dylan yelled.

"Hey! Where are you two? Come out!" Clyde shouted.

"Why the fuck did I break that goddamn walkie?" Dylan clenched his fists, breathing intensifying. "Fuck!"

"Hey, we'll find them. Don't worry."

Dylan walked along the edge of the pit. "Leah! Leah! Ariel! Where are you?"

"Dylan!"

Dylan's eyes adjusted in the darkness, Ariel emerged from the night, running toward him. She was alone. She was coming from a long way from where Dylan was. She'd looked panicked, and Dylan's mind continued to race away from him.

Leah is dead. She fell, and I'll never resolve what we could have saved.

This is all my fault.

"Ariel, fucking so glad you're safe," Dylan hugged Ariel as she came running.

Clyde caught up to them, stopping and meeting Ariel's line of sight. An awkward silence followed, approaching her, but he didn't appear concerned about her feelings. Everyone wanted to find Leah at all costs.

"Dylan, you have to save her. She fell in!" Ariel pointed into the worst place Dylan ever thought of entering. The emptiness that was before him made all previous chills comparable to a tingling sensation. The sight of the crater sized hole brought dread to him. Something unsettling beneath made his mind race, and he didn't want to find out what it was.

"What happened? How did she fall?" Dylan tried to keep his focus on his startled friend.

"I looked away from her for a second and then she screamed. It was the weirdest thing. It's like she floated down. It didn't look like she fell."

Dylan gazed back into the depths. He met Clyde's eyes, pondering his next move. How deep did it go? They could be going miles into the ground.

"Please, you have to hurry!" Ariel's raspy voice cracked. Ariel's deep dive into becoming her new self really resonating with Dylan. He respected the fact she was being who she thought she was meant to be.

"Have you both seen anything weird outside of Leah falling? Weird people doing unusual stuff?" Dylan looked on as the deformed emerged out from the shadows, gathering closer to the opening.

"Like what?" Ariel thought for a moment. Dylan could tell her expression was lost. She didn't seem to grasp the severity of Leah falling. She was as confused about everything as they were.

Some of the gathering had gotten closer.

"Look, I'm going to head down. We can talk after."

"Dylan, I think I found a way down!"

Clyde was kneeling in front of the pit. He shone his flashlight at the edge, finding a shallow drop they could jump down to.

Dylan walked over, looking into the pit being illuminated by the phone flashlight. The ground below was the remaining part of the fallen park. Heavy mounds of concrete with decorative brick towered atop a warped, rusted fountain. Several of the nozzles were bent downward and cracked from the base. The "PP" emblem was split almost in half like that of a broken heart.

The broken heart of the people who enjoyed Palisades Playland for all the years before the collapse.

"Keep the light going. I'll go first."

Ariel grabbed Dylan's arm.

"Please don't leave me by myself."

Dylan looked at Clyde. "Fine, Clyde will stay with you."

Ariel shook her head, looking at Clyde with disgust. "No, no, no."

"What?" Dylan looked up at her.

Then he remembered. Ariel had shown some disdain for Clyde. The hate and bigotry she'd faced in the short amount of time since transitioning was overwhelming. The last thing she needed was another dose of it during what should've been a fun night out with her best friend and boyfriend.

"Ariel, I'm sorry about what I said earlier. Can we just save Leah, and we can hash it out after?"

Dylan looked at Ariel's resistant expression. She nodded, despite not being comfortable with it.

"Clyde, help me down."

Ariel turned away, looking at the people emerging from the darkness. They kept their distance, not showing hostility. Ariel wasn't worried, but she was more alert.

"Stay back! These guys are ready to kick your ass!"

Dylan kneeled down near Clyde. "Help me down."

Dylan gripped Clyde's hand, descending into the shallow hole.

Clyde leaned in. "Glad she bought that bullshit apology. Be quick. I don't want to talk to her more than I have to."

Dylan didn't want to respond to his hurtful friend. Clyde played the victim for days and now he was being cruel toward Leah's friend, who didn't deserve it one bit as far as Dylan was concerned. He started to think that Clyde was projecting his anger at Ariel. Someone who fully emerged herself into accepting her reality and not letting people bring her down despite not being accepting of her. Clyde still managed to hide who he was, and Dylan couldn't help but think the anger was being mis-directed at Ariel, who didn't deserve it.

"Got it." Dylan kept his eyes on the ground as he dropped below.

He fell four or five feet. Much less traumatic than he had planned.

A faint applause echoed down into the darkness. He looked into the sky, seeing Ariel and Clyde's disconcerting expressions.

"What is that? What's going on?"

Ariel leaned in. "They're all… clapping."

Clapping? Did I fall into a trap?

Dylan pulled the flashlight from his carabiner. He clicked it on and was greeted by a dust cloud. Debris stirred up from his drop into the pit, clouded the air around him. He crept forward, pointing the light at the steps in front of him. He was careful walking over mounds of rubble in case the floor before him would pull him deeper.

"Dylan! Find anything?" Clyde shouted.

"Nothing yet. Really cloudy air down here." Dylan coughed as his steps kicked up more dust for him to breathe in.

Dylan walked with intense caution. The giant sink hole seemed to be endless, with darkness consuming every bit of area he could comprehend. The moonlight had shifted out of view, so if his flashlight decided to die, he would be doomed to the darkness.

"Clyde, do you have a better flashlight than your phone?" Dylan yelled.

No response. The darkness around the edge of the opening became much more apparent and the visibility of Ariel, Clyde, or any of the inhabitants was almost impossible.

"Clyde! Ariel!"

The flashlight clicked off.

"Shit! Shit!" Dylan proceeded to hit the flashlight over and over, trying to bring it back to life.

The darkness overwhelmed his level of comfort, unsettling him further. Dylan could never admit to being afraid of the dark, but in the instance of lack of control, he'd panic quickly.

Flashes of light came in and out of the black tube, giving him faint hope of regaining vision in the place that Dylan had no desire to be his crypt.

"Come on. Please. Please work." His whispers echoed like screams. The quick beams of light burst like dying fireflies.

The beam illuminated and stayed strong in the endless dark. Dylan pointed it left and right, seeing only the nothing offered before.

"Fucking thank god." Dylan wiped his forehead free of the sweat that was pouring into his eyes.

Someone stepped into the light, ruining Dylan's vision once again. A hand gripped Dylan's wrist.

"Hey, we won't be needing that where we're going."

"Leah?"

The dark was accompanied by a gathering atop the opening. Dozens of the inhabitants stood at the edge, looking down at Dylan and Leah.

"I understand now. We are meant for guiding these people to salvation. To the cathedral."

Dylan was thrown off by Leah; suddenly changing the dynamic of her mood after a night of bitterness and hostility. She'd flipped a switch to this warm girlfriend from early on in their relationship. He was curious as to why she'd become this welcoming suddenly.

"What are you talking about?"

"Just witness."

The inhabitants raised sharp objects to their throats. A mixture of blades, shards of glass, pieces of metal, and broken bottles. They all expressed joy, displaying big, bright smiles.

"LET US ALL AWAKE THE MESSIAH!" They shouted in unison.

Sharp objects opened throats like faucets of sacrificial blood. One by one, they dropped as their bodies were drained, giving their donation to their unknown god.

Bodies made wet thuds as their lives drained, colliding with the ground below. Blood splattered all over Dylan and Leah. Surrounded, Dylan didn't know whether to run and pull Leah away or to stay frozen in the current nightmare, consuming their death pit.

"What the fuck is happening, Leah?" Dylan shrieked as he looked around, seeing if the end of the terror was close or further from him.

"It's beautiful, isn't it, Dylan? Their sacrifice will allow us into the cathedral in a matter of hours."

"What the fuck are you talking about?"

A body fell at their feet, coating their chests and faces with a warm layer of devoted blood. The mangled face, still smiling, bent upward as the snapped neck bone dug out of the skin.

Dylan's eyes widened, staring in horror at his girlfriend, who only found solace in the mass suicide. They were distant, growing into different people from who they once were, but this new Leah was too far gone. Dylan needed to accept defeat in saving what they once had.

"Now we can be in love. Now we can be the king and queen of this new world."

Dylan couldn't stop himself when he ran toward where he dropped down. He climbed up on some mounds, trying to find a place to grip the cracked concrete he stood on earlier.

"Clyde! Help me!"

The echo of the final bodies hitting the ground near Leah were sloshing away like fallen, rotted pumpkins. Leah was still letting the orchestra of death serenade her holy site.

"Dylan, you can try to flee, but you will want this. You want you and I to work."

Dylan was lost in his thoughts. First Clyde, then a complete change from Leah? This new side of her frightened him. She was too calm in a moment of pure hysteria. He wasn't sure if he was ready to walk away entirely, but he didn't feel safe as bodies fell to his feet.

"Where are Clyde and Ariel?"

"They're being prepared."

Being prepared. Fuck, I'm going to die in here. She's possessed or something.

The ground rumbling had started. Leah stood still as Dylan tried to hold his ground on the unstable mound.

"Fuck, we're sinking again!"

"No. He is awake. At long last." Leah put her arms in the air, reaching into the sky with rejoice. "Now they can all join us!"

"Who? Who can join us?"

Dylan thought both he and Clyde had seen it all tonight, or at least what was left of defying reality for the evening.

Leah's feet left the ground, and she floated above him. It wasn't until this that he'd been the most wrong in his life about perceiving reality. All became lost in thought. Dylan couldn't fathom the slightest idea how she'd been able to do it, or if she was being helped by whatever was going on in this unusual presence tonight. She hovered above the hole Dylan climbed from, floating like a lone planet in an empty sky.

He thought back to the happiness of riding on the kid's coaster with his parents and being so thrilled that he was having the time of his life. His mom was often the thrill seeker in the family, while his dad was hardly capable of holding his vomit back after stuffing two corn dogs and a giant soda down his throat ten minutes before the ride.

He thought of as many memories that would triumph over the current bizarre reality that he was being trapped in. The thoughts, rich and full of joy, were long gone, just like the park he may never leave.

"Leah?"

The rumbling of the ground brought debris from the cracked concrete down. Mounds fell toward Dylan's location, growing the rubble taller. A concrete slab slid feet away from him and he waited for the opportunity to climb free and flee with his friend he hoped was still among the living.

He wasn't brave enough to stand up to her, and he wouldn't be brave enough to save her, either.

"I'm going, Leah. We're over. Done forever."

Her eyes were closed, but her smile grew as wide as her face allowed. Her teeth escaped her relaxed lips and grinned with intense serenity.

"They won't let you."

The concrete slab slid far enough for Dylan to climb up. He stood on it and the rumbling came to a halt. The ground he once stood on fell deeper into the Earth. The blackness grew, sending that familiar chill up Dylan's spine.

"They'll never let you leave. Ever."

A screech, similar to the one they heard earlier, echoed from the hole. Dark green limbs, similar to the ones he'd seen in the cavern ride, emerged like worms from moist dirt. They dug through the heavy ground, revealing spiked arms. They climbed like praying mantis.

The shrieks continued as they rose from the mounds, unearthing a horde of creatures coming to the surface.

Leah looked below at the monstrosities, looking pleased, like a mother releasing her pets to play upon their own space.

They climbed one another, growing higher in a mound of horrific teeth, a wide variety of eyes on each, and sharp claws that dug into one another while the toppling continued. Their slimy, dark green flesh caught the light from the moon, glistening and reflecting into Dylan's widened eyes.

Dylan climbed and ran for the gate.

"Clyde! Clyde, let's go! We have to leave right now!"

"Dylan! Dylan, help me!"

Dylan's surprised expression met Ariel's terrified one, screaming, as she was hauled away by the surviving inhabitants and dragged into the darkness of night.

"I'm coming!" Dylan ran after Ariel into the depths of the park. He ran through the maze of vendor carts and ticket booths. They weaved in and out, faster, fleeing Dylan as he was gaining. He kept an eye on her as he dodged the low planes of the children's rides. Ariel screamed louder, giving Dylan clues as to the direction he should pursue. He found himself growing further from the park entrance, and deeper in trouble.

It was like a trap he'd sprung and Leah was somehow involved with making it go that way.

Catching up and saving Ariel was only part of the problem. He still had to find Clyde.

Chapter Eleven

Dylan approached the perimeter fence and realized he had gone too far back. He was on the opposite side of where he wanted to be. Ariel's screams had grown faint and couldn't tell which direction he should be going.

"Ariel! Ariel, where are you?"

He hadn't seen any inhabitants for a while. Come to think of it, the last few were the ones taking Ariel into darkness.

The furthest ride from the entrance was a shallow roller coaster called *Little Speeder.* The ride had a few tight turns and was for teens who hadn't found their growth spurt yet. The ride sat within an oval opening just before the fence stopped the park from its line on the premises. Where the entrance sat just below the highway, this side was backed by miles of forest. It had the primary spot on a plot of land between the busy roads to the end of the city line, where the trees ran for further than most had ventured.

Some urban legends say the woods were haunted, bringing a curse to the park, which caused the collapse.

Dylan hadn't given any thought to any more of the nonsense of the park nor what actually did happen. He needed to save his friends and send Leah help whenever he got out.

"We will all protect the king. He must bring us down."

Inhabitants emerged from the carts of *Little Speeder*.

"Two for the Messiah and two for the new world."

"Guests of the king and queen will be the final gift from those who serve the Messiah."

More and more circled Dylan, pushing him further into deep inhabitant territory. He wasn't familiar with this part of the part anymore. He looked in all directions, overwhelmed by the mangled inhabitants.

"Hey, take a step back, everyone."

"All hail the k-"

A metal rod cracked against the face of the inhabitant closest to Dylan. Teeth flew out of his top lip, blood dripping down to his chin. He fell back, coughing on his blood. Several others came to his aid, bringing him back to his feet. He groaned in agony, but he did not wail or shout.

Clyde raised the metal rod high, pointing at each of the people.

"Back off, or more of you will be spitting out teeth like that asshole. Even if I have to swing my way out of here! Go!"

"We would never hurt him. He's too important."

"Sure, I'll believe you." Clyde rolled his eyes, emphasizing his sarcasm. "You're all fucking crazy. Go fuck off!"

The group walked away while supporting the wounded man. He gazed at Clyde before the darkness took him over again.

"Thanks. You didn't need to crack him open like that. I don't think they were going to kill me."

Dylan met Clyde's look, opening him up. He never really quite had the best judge of character that Clyde often teased him for.

"Yeah, Dylan. Maybe you really are royalty. Maybe they were going to take you to their throne made of pigeon bones and cardboard."

"Enough. Let's just find Ariel. Can we do that?"

Clyde pointed behind Dylan. "Found her."

Dylan turned to find a battered Ariel. Her face was bruised, and blood was gushing from her split eyebrow. Dylan was more worried about the deep gash on her shoulder.

Ariel's left hand gripped the soaked red top like she was holding her arm in place. Her entire right sleeve was soaked almost to the point of being black. Dylan caught her crying as she got closer. He had no idea that it wasn't exactly what he'd feared, staining Ariel's clothing.

It was something darker than blood.

"Ariel, what the fuck happened? Are you okay?"

Ariel's eyes met Dylan's. She'd grown exhausted, approaching morning by that time. Her visible face had already formed a discoloration from whatever aggression she'd endured. Dylan couldn't resist staring into her eyes.

Her eyes were black.

"Ariel? Are you okay?"

He leaned in, noticing a soft whisper she let out with short breaths.

"It isn't all of my blood. Whatever attacked me……wasn't human. Not fully anyway."

Dylan stepped back, examining her wounds. Her hand holding her shoulder was trembling. The breathing had gotten worse.

Dylan rested his hand on hers. "I need to look at it, Ariel. Want to check how bad it is."

Ariel nodded and released her hand. Her arm swung like a snapped rope, revealing the treacherous wound that had started on her upper back and across her chest. The gashes were deep. Spreading only inches from her throat.

"What happened?" Clyde asked.

"They took me inside a ride. Something cut me. It was slimy. It had some giant green arm."

Dylan recalled the slimy armed man in the cave. Was it the same one? Had there been a slew of these deformed beings walking around or hiding in the depths? He peered over at Clyde, who also was looking nervous.

"Could it be the same one from earlier?" Clyde whispered.

"I don't know. Something tells me there's more out there." Dylan peered over his shoulder. His nerves were all over the place.

"What do we do?" Ariel asked.

"Did you catch anything weird besides that thing that hurt you? Anything else weird at all?"

Ariel made eye contact. Her eyes were still haunting.

"Couple of weird people. Nothing bizarre until Leah fell in."

"Did she trip? Slip on something?" Clyde asked. "Leah doesn't strike me as clumsy enough to fall in."

Ariel gave Dylan a look that he'd never seen before. A realization of something she didn't quite understand herself.

"She was pulled down. It was like the pit wanted her."

The thunderous roar, the one that chilled Dylan's spine, echoed to the back of the park, where the three were hidden from the monstrosities.

Something was awake, and it was much bigger than any of them had witnessed so far.

Leah's voice, like a whisper in the wind, tickled Dylan's ear.

"It's almost time, my sweet. Let me show you what we need to do."

Dylan looked all around, yet no sign.

"Dylan, what's wrong?" Clyde spotted the panic in Dylan's eyes. He grabbed him, but Dylan wouldn't hold still. His panic was unraveling.

"Where is she? Where is Leah? Her voice……it's right next to me."

"Dude, we haven't seen her since our little argument earlier."

Ariel's blackened eyes locked on Clyde. "Little argument?"

"Sorry, does the truth hurt? There's nothing special about you now that you wear a skirt. You transitioned from dude to somewhat a girl. It's just a fact. No need to have your feelings-"

Ariel dove into Clyde. He hit the ground and was immediately thrown off by the attack. Ariel's build was similar to Clyde's scrawny frame.

She didn't speak while she her jagged nails ripped skin across his face. Blood rushed from the deep gashes as she scraped from his sideburn down to his chin. Clyde didn't say anything but screamed.

Clyde shoved her down. Ariel rushed into the darkness. Dylan glimpsed the panic in her blackened eyes while she fled.

"Fuck! My fucking face!"

The blood glistened in the moonlight's reflection. Clyde yelled while the warm fluid flowed from his wounds. He clenched as the pain rushed into his face with immense force.

"I'm going to kill that freak!" Clyde gripped the metal rod, standing.

"Clyde, hold on a second!" Dylan followed him closely.

Dylan had only seen Clyde this mad once or twice before. The first time was when Clyde, who often ran his mouth a bit too much in arguments, went off at someone in the college courtyard and walked out to find his car keyed. The second time was after his dad backhanded him during a heated argument. Again, because Clyde went way too far with words.

A different time of anger resonated in Clyde's eyes. It was violent. A lack of humanity with how he treated Ariel, and the impending doom brewing was even worse than his expression allowed him to show.

"She probably ran back to Leah. Fucking can't protect herself. Has to have her friend with a spine do it. Opposites really attract here, Dylan. Leah is a certified cunt. No wonder you can't stand up to her."

Dylan didn't want to admit the same thought he'd had ever since their relationship took a turn. Leah was much better at expressing herself. Even if it was aggressive or she just wanted to stir up trouble, Dylan was never any match against her verbal warfare.

"Dude, you don't have to be an asshole to me. Ariel didn't need to cut you up like that. But you also don't need to be rude to her like you have been all night."

Clyde dropped the rod, turning to Dylan. He smeared his fingers along his gashes and wiped the blood on Dylan's chest.

"A few hours ago, you were telling me to swallow your cock in the back of your car. When we did that a few weeks ago, I was so pleased that you came around and I was able to open up to someone. I was able to open up to my best friend. Now, after some stupid bitch who's been with you almost a decade less than me, comes in and changes you and I'm supposed to accept that. Fuck that. Fuck her for ruining the relationship with you. Fuck you for not having the fucking spine to do anything about it."

"Clyde—"

"And fuck that stupid tranny bitch. Why does she get to prance around town wearing her new self and I still have to be a faggot if I were to come out? She doesn't get to take away my happiness. I should be able to be gay just as much as she can cross dress! "

Clyde picked up the rod and waved it in Dylan's face. "If she wants reconstructive surgery, she will get it free of charge from me!" Dylan didn't have any words for all that. He was stunned, despite being used to Clyde speaking his mind.

"And one other thing......" Clyde grabbed Dylan's face, slipping his tongue between his friend's lips. Blood dripped onto their lips, glazing their heated embrace with his warm fluids. Neither of them broke or resisted. Clyde's confidence turned Dylan on. He grew further confused with his sexuality, but it wasn't foreign to him anymore. This night was all over the place for Dylan's sanity, but he was certain that some lingering sexual feelings for his friend had broken through. If he got out of the park alive tonight, he'd certainly explore the idea of tasting one another without the layer of booze to disrupt their bodies embracing.

Clyde waved the rod back and forth, walking away.

"Try to stop me, but Ariel is getting something from me."

"Clyde? Clyde!"

Clyde power-walked ahead of Dylan, ignoring Dylan's words. It would lead to a wise choice of rational thinking and keeping his cool, but Dylan accepted that Clyde's anger was unbreakable. Knowing his projected anger got the better of Clyde, he feared for Ariel. He wanted to do everything he could to find and save her from Clyde's burning rage.

Dylan grew more nervous. His growing anxiety from the night's stress was overwhelming him. He'd lost his girl, seen death, and now had to fight his friend from becoming a murderer.

Inhabitants followed, staring at Dylan's violent companion. They were aware of something Dylan still didn't quite understand. He hadn't been listening to their words, despite hearing them recite nonsense all night.

What did it all mean? Where was the grand cathedral they were all talking about? Was everyone else just really into some cult, or was the drug epidemic spreading among these people living in this abandoned amusement park?

"Hey, hey you. Can you help me?" Dylan pointed at a woman who had half of her left cheek missing. He didn't really care how she'd lost it. He'd concluded it was probably from either extensive drug use or from her sacrifice earlier in the evening. Somehow, a lot of inhabitants wandered still despite watching so many fall to their deaths.

She walked over with reveling excitement. She appeared pleased, almost as if she were grateful to be in the presence of fame.

"Yes, how may I serve you?" She curtsied, showing deep admiration for Dylan.

"No need for the formalities, I just-"

She placed her filthy finger on Dylan's lips, trying to ignore the grime caked on her finger. Dylan backed away, trying his hardest not to gag in front of her. Her skin matched the remaining teeth she still had, blackened and almost out of her mouth.

"Nonsense. You are the new royalty, my dear. You will bring us to salvation!" The black teeth rose from the smiling lips. Dylan had to fight the urge not to gag in her presence. Her mouth was foul, reeking of infection, poisonous saliva, and expired food, which probably consisted of the majority of her diet. Dylan had never been in the presence of a viler person before.

"You're mistaken. I am no leader. Nor a king."

She pointed at Clyde, who was getting away from Dylan's sight. "Your turning point is here. His fate, and yours, are at a crossroads. Go, save the kingdom!"

She patted Dylan on the back, and he took off running.

Dylan didn't look back. Nor did he have a reason to. He was far beyond over this bizarre nightmare going on around him.

The return to the opening was a shocking sight. The creatures that emerged from the hole were drenched in dark green slime. Limbs and spiked appendages of all sizes were pointed toward their queen, hovering in the air.

Leah was looking down at her small army of monsters that had ascended from the depths of the park.

Dylan realized they were covered in pieces of flesh.

Flesh of the inhabitants that had offered themselves as sacrifice decorated the creatures. Several used the skin of the arms as decorative pieces, or they accompanied the torn flesh with pieces of bone for armor. Peeled faces being used as masks. Sharpened bones with the hands and feet still attached were held firmly. Each creature had their own tailored decor or armor. They were ready for any challenge brought their way.

Clyde stared at Ariel. She was blocked by a group of armored creatures.

"My dear Dylan. Come join me. " Leah's voice was soft, welcoming in this confrontational encounter.

Dylan looked at his floating girlfriend, twenty or so feet in the air. Had she dropped from that height, the darkness of the fallen earth would swallow her once again.

"Leah, please come down. How are you even doing that?" Dylan wiped the thick sweat and grime from his forehead.

"My love, the beings from the other world granted me the power to bring them back home. We will be royalty in the new home. We can rekindle our broken love. Live our lives as their leaders as soon as we can bring them to the cathedral."

A faint applause started in the distance. He looked behind him and dozens of inhabitants gathered among the creatures and opening. They kept their distance from the gathering below Leah.

"Once Clyde takes Ariel's life, it will set the final piece in motion. We can go home."

"Go home? Leah, we live a few miles away. Let's go home now. We can fix this. Clyde and I can figure out our tension, and he will apologize to Ariel."

Leah opened her hand in Dylan's direction. His stress faded away as weightlessness took over and he flew from his feet and soared into the air in front of Leah. Her eyes were almost as black as Ariel's were.

"You mean run off and start your homosexual life with Clyde? I caught you two by the car and I could overhear your heart beating for him. Ever since that hole swallowed me, I'm aware of things, even from a distance. It's important that I do acquire this information. It gives me closure."

Tears ran down Dylan's face. He had trouble looking Leah in her eyes. "What happened, Leah? You aren't the person who fell in."

Leah held Dylan's face. Warmth radiated from her for the first time in a long time. Like the love they had on their first date. It was the butterflies he had when they first realized their mutual affection for one another. He'd grown to almost hate her this evening, but the connection she returned to his heart in that moment seemed like it would last forever.

"I woke up, Dylan. I want you to open your eyes with me. We don't have to try to wake up here and do this over and over. We can wake up as the royalty these fine denizens perceive us. Become happy and have it everlasting for the rest of our lives. The rest of infinity, if we want it. Don't you want that?"

"Hey, sorry to break up the little spooky love story, but what's the deal? Am I doing this or what?" Clyde asked. He tightened his grip on the rod, wrapping both hands around it like he was ready to crack a ball over the distant fence.

"What the hell is he talking about?" Dylan asked. "Did you give him permission to kill Ariel?"

"She is a worthy sacrifice. Her death will solidify our devotion to the Messiah."

"Wait. This isn't right." Dylan turned to Clyde and froze. He couldn't go down to his friend to stop him from doing something he'd never return from.

"Clyde! Don't you do anything stupid!"

"Leah! Come down here and help me!"

Leah didn't break eye contact with Dylan. She was ready to witness everyone below her make their next move.

"It's okay. They aren't worthy of our world. Distractions among our time in this dimension."

"Leah, I understand you're having a change of heart and righteous about having powers, but these are our friends we're talking about. Our GOOD friends. Our best friends. Please-"

"Your words hold no value. The severity of your feelings for Clyde changes things. What you did with him…… And don't think for one second I haven't forgotten about it."

Dylan's breath escaped him. *How could she have seen? What exactly did she catch them doing?* It was only a matter of time before something would have exploded from Clyde's lips or she would have seen something else between them. Dylan wasn't gay, nor did he want to give off that impression. He still felt something for Leah, despite being sexually involved with Clyde. He wanted nothing more than to make it work with her, and he'd gone above and beyond to prove that. After tonight, if they all went home, it would involve big changes to everyone involved.

"Leah, I-"

"In his basement, in the car minutes before my scream, and that kiss between you two."

How did she discern our kiss? How did she find out about these things while inside the park? Where did she obtain powers like this?

Leah's hands fell over Dylan's eyes, showing him glimpses of her visions earlier that night, and seeing everything her perception had been granted access to. Her scream was the release of rage, letting go of the built-up tension she held down after first seeing Clyde swallow Dylan's dick. She only realized how to confront him until right now.

The ground rumbled. Leah's eyes rolled back to reveal an all-white gaze returning to Dylan. He floated with helpless surrender. She was overpowering him, and he couldn't break through to her and stop his friend again from making another mistake.

"Clyde, do as you must."

Clyde looked up at Leah with a grinning satisfaction. He tossed the rod from hand to hand, walking toward Ariel. The inhabitants pushed Ariel in front of him. Terror flooded her eyes as his maniacal smile beneath his blood-soaked face lit him up with joy. He'd been ready for this, and no one was going to stop him.

"Do it with passion!"

"Clyde, don't you fucking do this! It's only going to hurt you! Please! Please, we can talk about everything!" Dylan's voice exploded from the depths of his throat.

Clyde's attention never left Ariel. His lips moved, and Dylan was well aware of what he said. The words echoed in his head despite being barely audible. The night grew colder with the words.

"I only need her death."

Bam!

The rod cracked against Ariel's face. Her eyebrow split open again and dripped warm crimson down her face.

Her fingertips, clenching her wound tight, were quickly soaked. A muffled response came from her lips. Clyde leaned in to listen.

"I didn't quite catch that, freak."

Clyde swung again, catching the side of her face. Her cheek tore open, oozing blood from the fresh wound. Her lips leaked the liquid that was quickly filling her mouth.

"LEAH! HELP ME, PLEASE!"

Dylan gripped Leah, still haunted by the whites of her eyes. Her grin stretched from ear to ear. She was in a trance that Dylan couldn't break.

"Leah, you have to let me down and I need to stop Clyde. You don't understand!"

"It is you who doesn't understand."

Dylan's head turned against his will. Leah's strength grip him, turning him away from her and forced to view his friend unravel. Ariel's face was gushing blood from multiple spots. Her stance was wobbly, swaying from side to side. She blocked her face as much as she could.

"How do you like the idea of dying in front of all of these people, you fucking mutant?" Clyde's swings splashed crimson with every contact of the rod. Ariel's clothes were black, like in the darkest part of dawn. Sunrise was upon them, yet not the slightest bit of light was left inside Clyde. Dylan had lost him. However the night turned out, his friend was beyond saving for good.

Tears filled Dylan's eyes. "Please. He's going to kill her."

Leah's eyes came back to her hazel glow. She smiled at Dylan once again.

"It's soon to be complete."

Dylan swung his fist into Leah's nose.

They were suddenly falling.

Dylan had broken whatever type of power she had over him. He was falling rapidly and hoped the person beneath him would break his fall.

A loud snap reverberated while Dylan collided with an inhabitant. His ankle was twisted, but someone else's neck was bent downward, sunk past the collarbone. The man dropped face first into the pit.

He looked up to Clyde, breathing heavily, drenched in Ariel's blood. He hadn't convinced himself he should look at what remained of her. He was drawn to his friend or what was left of him. He thought back to laughing among friends who'd spent all night driving around, about the many times Clyde mouthed off in class for a rise out of the teacher, or just simply made a fond memory alone with his friend.

The Clyde that Dylan befriended had diminished. Madness had embodied where Clyde stood. He was nothing more than the monster that always lived inside of him.

"Good. You did well, Clyde." Leah approached him with gratitude. They both looked down at Ariel.

Dylan finally did, too.

Most of Ariel's face was a mangled mess of teeth and fluids leaked from her left eye. Her jaw dangled from its battered hinges, revealing one or two remaining front teeth that survived. Her head was split down to her skull, where her hair parted.

Ariel's mouth was open. Dylan recalled her screaming while she was being killed, but he didn't have the slightest idea what she was saying while he was struggling to break through to Leah.

More people and creatures had gathered since Dylan had arrived back at the opening. Something else was due to happen in the next few moments.

"You did very well." Leah's hand gently lifted Clyde's chin. Their eyes met in a blissful rejoice of success. Ariel's death was something Clyde needed to achieve. Something deep within him emerged from the hate he held dear after so many years.

"She was a distraction. Now she is no more."

Clyde turned to Dylan. He wiped Ariel's splatter from his own wound. His smile was unsettling to Dylan. It was not the smile Dylan liked to earn from inappropriate jokes or crude remarks to one another. He was fully evolved to such creatures they endured tonight.

"Dylan, happen to catch that? Leah is finally coming to our side. Even got to rid ourselves of a pest. I'd say it was a successful night. Worked out after all!"

Clyde tossed the rod on Ariel's remains.

Leah's hands moved to Clyde's cheeks. She was careful not to graze his face, touching his thick wound.

"All distractions must end for us to reach the cathedral."

"Right." Clyde approached Dylan, but stopped when he couldn't walk any further.

"What's happening? I can't move anymore."

Dylan immediately thought of Leah's powers. *She's doing something!*

"Clyde......" Dylan pointed at Leah, while the remaining inhabitants formed a close circle around the three.

Clyde looked at Leah's chilling expression. Her eyes were rolled back in her head, and she had her wide grin on. She held her hand toward Clyde, as if she were gripping him in place.

"Leah? What the fuck are you doing? Let go of me." Clyde flexed, but it was of no use. He couldn't budge even the slightest inch.

"Clyde." Leah's voice dropped several octaves. His eyes widened. He was showing more fear than he had all night.

"ALL distractions……must end!"

Chapter Twelve

As hard as Clyde pulled in any direction, he was frozen in place. His veins bulged with every attempted pull, giving every effort to pull out of the position he was being held.

"Leah, what are you doing? Tonight, has gone far enough and we need to leave here right this fucking instant. Whatever you need me to say about Ariel……I'll say it. We can walk away right now."

The creatures shrieked in unison at Leah's seldom response.

"Dude, control your fucking woman!" Clyde directed all his anger at Dylan.

Dylan was frozen and helpless, like his captive friend. Leah was conducted this final performance and disregarded her deceased friend. The final piece was Clyde, yet Dylan nor Clyde had any idea what that entailed.

"Leah, please!" Dylan put his remaining efforts into his plea to Leah. Her focus was unscathed.

Leah's eye contact broke and peered into the crowd of onlookers. Between inhabitants and creatures, she hadn't picked a particular individual to focus on. Her eyes scanned everyone as she avoided eye contact with Dylan and Clyde. Dylan couldn't help but gaze at the anticipated search for something else to come aid the dread they endured.

Leah's finger pointed to a being with jagged teeth poking from its cheek and heavy claws emerging from its oversized limbs. "My loyal servant. You first."

It charged at Clyde, lunging into the air far above his head.

It landed behind him, dragging its claws down Clyde's back. The shirt and skin tore with one clean drag and the red started flowing.

Clyde's scream echoed throughout the empty park.

Despite a presence in the park more than the night permitted, the sun still hadn't risen. The darkness seemed to be infinite, trapping the group and the new inhabitants in blackness that never grew to light.

"Fucking do something, Dylan! Save me!" Clyde wailed as tears flowed down his face.

"You. Take your piece."

Another creature lunged at Clyde. The claws ripped at the flesh of his upper leg. Skin peeled from the muscle and dripped down his leg. He cried louder as his shoes quickly stained red.

"Dylan......."

"Clyde, I can't do anything to overpower her. She won't stop."

Clyde chuckled. The tears flowed more.

"This is exactly why she is ahead of you. You've never had the balls to stand up to her. You were never strong enough to express your feelings!"

Another creature slashed Clyde's arm open. His muscles exposed the flesh tore and blood soaked down to his wrist.

"It should have been us. We'd be better off, and we'd be back home already. Now, because of her, take a look at how ruined we all are."

Dylan tried his best to focus on Clyde's words as if he was dying alongside his friend, who was being ripped apart and split open. He caught Leah say "two at once" and his stomach dropped to the lowest point it could.

One inhabitant and another creature slashed into Clyde's chest and stomach. His shirt quickly soaked through, and he was growing weaker with every wound. His lips were coated with a fresh layer of red as his mouth filled with blood.

"You were never the man you needed to be. For that, I'll never be able to love the one I wanted."

Dylan sobbed at this point. Leah was smiling as Clyde inched closer to death. The onlookers were watching with joy as the public execution was nearly complete.

"Leah, finish me off, you wretched cunt. The sooner I'm away from you, the better."

Dylan forced himself to turn to Leah.

An inhabitant stepped forward after Leah pointed at him. He drew a blade from his pocket and stood behind Clyde.

"I'll make sure your bed is made in hell, Dylan."

Clyde fell to the ground as his restraint was lifted. His loose skin flapped as he collided with the concrete. He sobbed as the pressure against his open wounds.

The man grabbed Clyde by the hair and dragged the blade from his lip up to his forehead. The screams didn't slow down, the skin tearing like a wet napkin. As blood filled his eyes and mouth, the volume dampened.

Clyde's face separated from his head with each firm pull. The blade dropped to the ground as the hairline separated from the scalp and the remaining piece peeled off the mangled face. Clyde's only noise was a moist gurgle as blood took over the orifices of his now ruined expression.

A loud, wet slap resonated when Clyde's corpse touched the ground. Small streams fled from his open wounds, gathering into a pool that surrounded him like a round carpet.

Leah put her hands down and the thunderous roar and cheer of the creatures echoed in the silence.

"As you all are aware, not everyone can come on this journey. We do, however, applaud your devotion."

Her fingers snapped, and the creatures ripped through the remaining inhabitants. Blood sprayed in all directions while the screams filled the night air. Fingers were scattered and limbs were torn away from bodies like loose band aids. Blood soaked the base of Dylan's shoes. He was frozen in place and sobbing as the mass murder in front of him took all of his strength away. He turned his head toward where he remembered entering from. If he made it past the small carnival booths, went past a few smaller rides, he could clear the gate and return to his car.

He didn't have to do this anymore. Alone, but he could survive and live another day.

The screaming ended and Dylan looked back at a smile glowing on Leah's face. He could tell she had the ability of looking through him, reading everything going on in his brain.

"Dylan, my love……" The words processed in his brain, but he chose not to listen. He just took off into the night. The absence of light was his only ally. He had no idea of her further capabilities, but he was ready to leave this night in the depths of his memory.

Dylan didn't bother turning back for reassurance of his safety or impending danger. He just kept pushing forward into the darkness. He passed the booths, ran around the entrance for the Ferris wheel, and finally the chain-link fence gave him solace he would make it to safety. He closed in, not looking back. He dreaded seeing something worse than anything the night had already scared him with.

He approached the entrance and froze. Locked in his stance, just like Clyde. He tried to flex, reaching for the fence, but it was no use. He couldn't remove his arms from his sides, no chance of a grip at all.

"Please, Leah, don't do this!"

Nothing but the deadly night responded. His current position wasn't accompanied by any creatures or Leah doing anything ominous to him.

Dylan went airborne. He flew high in the sky, way above the park. It was looking like a faint object in the distance. Higher and higher he climbed, and only his screams echoed in the quiet night air.

"Oh shit! Oh shit, please! Please, Leah! Stop! Stop this!"

Higher, almost at the distance of looking out of a plane window. He was petrified. At this distance, he was petrified of facing death at full speed.

Dylan was hit with an abrupt stop. He levitated in the air just below the clouds. He admired the entire park and analyzed its abandoned beauty.

He pondered if this was his final moment. If Leah's grip around him let go, he would live his final seconds plummeting to the world below him. His tears dripped from his face and vanished into the air beneath him.

Then the ground moved beneath him. The standing rides lifted from something enormous moving below the soil.

Support beams dipped below, toppling to the ground. The loud rumbling at his height could only mean that whatever this was moving was bigger than anything living on Earth.

The cracking concrete all led to the opening. A small gathering formed around Leah. They circled the hole and raised their arms.

Dylan descended toward them at a slow pace, relieving his fear of plummeting like a meteor. His breathing intensified as he was drawing closer to whatever they had summoned.

Dylan was at ease being back at a normal height.

"Stop this, Leah!"

She turned, looking deep into Dylan's eyes. She stood between pools of their friends' blood, perfectly synchronized. Dylan thought the innocent look on Leah's face was like the ones she gave early in their relationship.

Before they had too much on their plates, got involved with Clyde, and were less troubled to the point of no return.

"My love. Meet our Messiah."

The cement exploded from the edge of the opening. A monstrous claw, towering over Dylan's height, came bursting out into the sky, slapping down on the concrete. Following, a tentacle of equal size and proportion slapped down on the creatures, pulling them into its heavy suctions and removing their intestines from their bodies. A roar followed as several more appendages emerged from the depths. The limbs seemed to be endless, coiling and hitting the ground all around the grounds opening.

"You first, my king," Leah said.

The goliath creature climbed up from the ground below. Dylan had lost count of the number of eyes sprouting from the black skin. It resembled the features of a massive tarantula with the number of eyes and appendages it had yet was flexible and could move like an octopus. The skin was almost scale-like showing textured patterns similar to a lizard. The roar, too giant for its body that towered almost eighty feet, reminded Dylan of a dinosaur with some enhancements.

The roar echoed in the air again, looking at the sky while it expelled its giant sound.

It looked Dylan in the eye. It reduced its aggression, like a horse finally caught by its trainer. Despite being from another world and colossal against Dylan, its eyes offered a sense of peace and trust for him. As the Messiah drew closer, Dylan pondered why it wasn't slowing down. The being lowered its head, and an orifice opened like a giant blowhole. The hole opened in the form of a human body. Dylan hoped it wasn't meant for him.

He suddenly flew into place, half of his body sunk into the gelatin like texture of the monster and the other half facing the other side of its nostrils.

Dylan tried his best to pull free from the swampy body, but it remained hopeless. His efforts drowned like his body beneath the monster. His peripherals offered a glimpse of Leah floating toward a similar fate.

"Leah, what is happening?"

"The queen joins the king, and we are welcomed into the grand eternal realm."

Leah sunk in as well, embracing the submergence like she stepped into a hot tub. Her eyes locked onto Dylan's.

"Now. We are ready."

"Ready for-"

The Messiah let out the roar that shook the remaining courage from Dylan. It pierced his ears from the sheer volume and magnitude it harnessed in its vocal cords. The sound vibrated more than Dylan could withstand.

How is no one hearing this? How are no fire trucks or police or fucking SWAT coming to investigate what is happening?

"Dylan, once the connection is complete, nothing on Earth can stop us."

"Did you listen to what I was thinking? Can this thing read our minds?"

Leah's hand slid through the skin like wading water. She gripped Dylan's.

"In here, we are one thought. One body. One power."

"Where are we-"

She squeezed Dylan's arm. "It's time."

Two massive tentacles reached into the sky.

"By the devotion of man, running thick in human blood, can the Messiah return to the place of worship. With the unity of the royal, human king and queen, may the doors open and devotion inside the cathedral begin."

The tentacles drew a trapezoid shape in the air. As they drew, an absence formed. The lines were immersive with a glowing black shine. The colossal size of the shape was scaled to the Messiah's body.

A doorway. Big enough to swallow the monstrosity.

"Leah, let this thing kill me. I don't want to be here. I don't want to go."

"The king and queen will live in sempiternal. The Messiah can live again, being the altar we need to pray upon so we can prey upon those who mean us extinction."

The trapezoid's glow shined through the thickening lines.

The Messiah's claw reached up and pushed the trapezoid into the abyss behind.

The world fell silent. The sun rose and dawn welcomed Dylan's hopeful, absent stare. He smiled, knowing that sunlight meant the nightmare was over and he could wake up.

He would let his mind succumb to the alarm and he could start his day and put this awful nightmare, one he'd laugh about with Clyde later, behind him.

The Messiah went airborne, and the creatures attached themselves as they entered the trapezoid. Dylan's vision beyond the eyes and head of the monster was limited, nor did he want to witness the world he loved vanish forever.

He took in the sights ahead. Deep, vibrant, glowing orbs surrounded him in the blackness.

They glowed with a silver aura, reflecting one another like a room full of mirrors. No sound was present on the abysmal journey.

They traveled at a rapid speed, but he had no concept of how long they were traveling for or how far they were going.

In the distance, an absence surrounded them again. The stars were fewer and far between until there was nothing.

Black engulfed them and nothing else.

Leah met Dylan's eyes.

Leah as she was when they entered the park. Cold, heartless, and seldom affectionate.

Tears ran down her face. "I hated you when we got to that park, but I'd take it all back right now. I'd let it all go to have this again."

"What are you talking about? You aren't yourself."

Leah's makeup ran with her sobbing. "I wasn't me after I came out of that hole. I don't understand who I was. But I'm me again, and I'm dreading what we are doing."

Dylan had nothing left. He let it all go. They looked at one another, emptying all emotions they could, considering it was the final moments of their lives.

"I love you, Dylan. Forever."

"I love you too, Leah. Until forever."

The bright glow distracted them. Ahead of them was a tall cathedral in the distance. The doors swung open.

The great building reflected with a dark glow. A reflective dark green color danced around the outside. It was floating in the air like a dazzling jewel on display.

They'd never seen a green like this for a place of worship.

"It's stunning. It looks like it's alive."

And it was. They were within feet of the building when they admired the entire building was made of the creatures they'd encountered.

The Messiah entered the door, and the creatures released. They climbed into the cathedral among the other living.

The entire building was made of these beings. The walls, stained glass, altar, even the pews were of living creation. Besides Dylan, Leah, and the newly returned celestial being, everything living was one unified place of worship.

Claws and arms moved all around while being serenaded with an orchestra of wailing and shrieking.

Dylan followed the path to where he was going. In front of the altar was a pair of thrones lined with human bones. A collection he guessed from the numerous sacrifices of the night and collected deaths over the years. Above those, towering hundreds of feet in the air in the tower above the altar, was an opening which Dylan assumed was for their shuttle from a monstrous origin.

The Messiah stopped in front of the thrones, and the two bodies separated. Dylan and Leah landed on their feet and examined their own bodies. Shocked by their journey, they were amazed traveling beyond a reality they'd ever experienced didn't leave them with any injuries or ailments.

Dylan looked around the cathedral, terrified of the movements around him. He looked at Leah, finally calm after everything that had happened.

"Are you still scared?" he reached for her hand, gently holding her fingers.

Leah couldn't keep her eyes off of the thrones. She shook her head. "I was, but I'm at ease here. Something makes it all okay."

"What do you think it is?" Dylan asked.

"Being with you. After all, this is all we are. I think our friends distracted us from......us. These things got it before we did. We have to make it work. Nothing else comes after."

The Messiah had climbed high in the air, mounting on its slot above the altar. It looked down as it latched into place, being housed and held by the hundreds if not thousands of loyal servants that made this place of worship whole.

"We can make whatever this is work. Our love will keep us immortal. I'm so sorry, Leah."

"I'm sorry too."

Leah reached up to kiss Dylan. He held her tightly as he reciprocated.

The roars from within echoed around the great width of the building.

Leah and Dylan finished their kiss and realized the inhabitants had been kneeling in the pews in front of them. All the mangled and tattered faces that lit up with bright smiles.

One man stood. "At long last. The king and queen are home!"

Cheering followed.

"Leah, if we are royalty, is that thing their God?"

The creatures fell silent as the inhabitants stood up. The attention fell to Dylan, who froze like he asked the wrong question.

The same inhabitant pointed at the Messiah.

"*We...... weeeereee...... long before god. Weeeeee... will be...... long afffterrrrrrr!*"

The eruption of applause and cheers followed.

Dylan held Leah's hand and walked her up to her throne. She sat, and he followed.

The warmth of human bone resonated up their spines.

They had gained a newfound love for one another.

Neither Dylan nor Leah had the words for their positions. The cheering and shrieks serenaded them for more they could comprehend.

All they could do was wait for the next part of their fate to unravel, as they embraced the love that they convinced themselves kept them safe.

Love would bind them in their new dimension.

Epilogue

The demolition crew was flabbergasted to find the state of Palisades Playland in the early hours before the machinery would deconstruct the fallen amusement park. The unstable opening in the ground had nearly doubled in size and made most of the property further unstable. Some of the bigger roller roasters had toppled over, sending pieces of track beyond the grounds. Most of the structures within proximity of the hole had been swallowed. Several crew members spotted sections of blood but couldn't determine the origin.

Investigators didn't recover any body parts. The recovery of anything swallowed was determined lost and would eventually be buried deeper, as the remaining structures would be carefully demolished, as the ground wasn't safe enough to allow a proper crew to continue. Many people were baffled as the news spread. No reported earthquakes or other natural disasters that would cause such a massive shift of the grounds. The property was condemned by the local council soon after.

As the ongoing investigation continued, very few people were able to catch a glimpse of the sunken grounds. They began to drift away from the onlooking crowd as little excitement would happen on demolition day. Watching things topple to the ground wasn't a dream that would be fulfilled. By the following nightfall, one or two watchers who hoped they'd catch some action stood nearby on the sidewalk.

All those who were excited about the park coming down for the future development of something better were disappointed and angry. Palisades Playland had fallen into a memory without the excitement of watching it collapse.

Swallowed forever in time and no one could give a sure answer as to how. Somewhere, deep in the annals of time and space, some people got to witness what really happened. A final memory in Palisades Playland was one the world would forget, but a few would worship for eternity.

Acknowledgements

My readers. Every time I see someone new reading my book, I'm so pleased to welcome you into my worlds. To my readers who have been with me, the encouragement keeps me alive and going. You are the pillars of my drive. I have so much more to show you!

Author friends, old and new. It's been a wild three years. I'm deeply honored to know so many of you. Megan Stockton, Daniel Volpe, John Wayne Comunale, Tim Meyer, Frank Endler, JC Walsh, Scott Cole, Adam Cesare, Jamie Zaccaria, and so many others. See you soon!

To my editor, Candace Nola. Thank you for your devotion, friendship, advice, and tolerance. You make this entire author life seem like it's normal.

My loving mother. Thank you for always reading and sharing your devotion to things you would never read otherwise. I'm so proud to be your son.

To my beloved wife, Nadia. Thank you for all that you do and tolerate when I drag you with me in this horror obsession. I will love you forever.

To my friends, who constantly ask when I'm getting that Stephen King money. Thank you for the push. I promise I'm working on it!

To you, whoever you are reading this right now. Yes, you! I hope you liked this book. If not, I'll have more for you to give me another chance. I appreciate you anyway.

ABOUT JOSEPH PESAVENTO

Joseph has been writing since he was eleven years old. He was inspired by the Nickelodeon show Doug because he kept a journal at the same age. Since then, Joseph has written numerous short stories and found interest in writing screenplays. Fast forward to his college graduation. Three short films written, produced, and directed with some film festival recognition. His love for writing stories, creating worlds, and developing characters to both admire and detest flourished as he never stopped creating.

Joseph branched off from screenplays when his ideas broadened beyond what the screen could portray. With a collection of stories in his archive and several novels in the works, there's no telling what will come from his mind and expand onto the pages. With each piece of writing released, Joseph is constantly expanding his creativity while interacting with fellow writers, documenting his journey, reading, and filling his mind with more inspiration for the next story.

www.ingramcontent.com/pod-product-compliance
Lightning Source LLC
LaVergne TN
LVHW041711060526